SALUTE MY SAVAGERY

Fumiya Payne

Lock Down Publications and Ca$h
Presents
Salute my Savagery
A Novel by *Fumiya Payne*

Fumiya Payne

Lock Down Publications
Po Box 944
Stockbridge, Ga 30281

Visit our website @
www.lockdownpublications.com

Copyright 2023 by Fumiya Payne
Salute my Savagery

Lock Down Publications
Like our page on Facebook: Lock Down Publications @
www.facebook.com/lockdownpublications.ldp
Book interior design by: **Shawn Walker**
Edited by: **Jill Alicea**

Stay Connected with Us!

Text **LOCKDOWN** to 22828 to stay up-to-date with new releases, sneak peaks, contests and more...
Thank you.

Submission Guideline.

Submit the first three chapters of your completed manuscript to ldpsubmissions@gmail.com, subject line: Your book's title. The manuscript must be in a .doc file and sent as an attachment. Document should be in Times New Roman, double spaced and in size 12 font. Also, provide your synopsis and full contact information. If sending multiple submissions, they must each be in a separate email.

Have a story but no way to send it electronically? You can still submit to LDP/Ca$h Presents. Send in the first three chapters, written or typed, of your completed manuscript to:

LDP: Submissions Dept
Po Box 944
Stockbridge, Ga 30281

DO NOT send original manuscript. Must be a duplicate.

Provide your synopsis and a cover letter containing your full contact information.

Thanks for considering LDP and Ca$h Presents.

ACKNOWLEDGEMENTS

First and foremost, all praise to the Most High, for without His exceptional patience and undeserved mercy, I'm certain my journey would've long ago ended.

Ca$h…my deepest gratitude for offering me an outlet, and I can personally attest to the solidity of your character. You taught me that words are worthless when actions don't align.

To the select few men behaving as true Kings…carry on. and may you find the courtesy to correct the flawed characters of your fellow peers. It's said you can't be a boss until you've created one. So what your count read?

A double salute to my sisters surviving the struggle. No matter how difficult life seems, please don't ever lose sight of your self-worth. Because what is the strongest piece on a chess board? The QUEEN, which means the game is yours. So in the words of Glorilla, "Let's Go!"

Fumiya Payne

Chapter 1

Inside a tinted Dodge Charger, three darkly-clothed demons wordlessly rode through the hazardous streets of Detroit, Michigan. Armed with fully automatics and armor-piercing ammo, they were moments away from executing the first of several heinous acts.

Seated in the van's backseat was the trio's eldest, 25-year-old Kavoni McClain. Recently released from a maximum-security prison, beneath his Kevlar vest was a chiseled frame that was sprayed like a subway in Harlem.

Up front in the passenger seat was Kavoni's most loyal and trusted friend, Puma. Standing 5'5" and 130 pounds, she favored the female artist, Ella Mai. But in spite of her angelic appearance, Puma was deadly enough to cut a man's throat with just a blade of grass.

And behind the wheel was Kavoni's younger brother, King. Aside from his blonde dreads, both siblings shared the same cinnamon hue, handsome features, and the large tattoo of an N.F.L. logo across their throats. An abbreviation for NEVER FORSAKE LOVE OR LOYALTY, the logo not only represented their belief system, but "The N.F.L." was also the moniker of their murderous gang, who were in a league of their own.

Turning off 7 Mile road, King made a right onto Hayes and purposely parked near the end of the block.

"Wait till you hear the fireworks," Kavoni reminded him as he and Puma slipped on backpacks and adjusted ski masks over their faces. "Then count to ten and pull around to Westphalia."

Kavoni handed Puma a gas can before they exited the car and marched between two vacant houses. As they crossed an alleyway and approached a tall privacy fence, Kavoni reached inside his backpack and removed a white package. He opened it to reveal a thick slab of meat and tossed it over. They could hear a dog greedily chewing, then seconds later came a soft thud as the canine lifelessly collapsed to the ground. The meat had been laced with a deadly dose of fentanyl.

After smoothly scaling the fence, Kavoni crouched down to watch the windows of the tan house before calling for the gas can. Upon joining him in the backyard, Puma removed an FN-P90 from her backpack and stood guard as Kavoni splashed the back of the house with five gallons of jet fuel. Because it burned much quicker and hotter than regular gasoline, Kavoni poured a trail of the fuel in the grass as he backpedaled toward the fence. Then, before climbing back over, he flicked a lighter and flung it.

WOOSH!

As the grass went up in flames and began slithering toward the house, Kavoni and Puma ran to get in position.

It wasn't long before the occupants of the house realized it was on fire. With no choice but to exit through the front door, the first few out were literally dismembered by bullets bigger than AA batteries.

The others instantly realized it was an ambush and hugged the floor. But with the raging flames only feet away, it was either fry in a furnace or face the firing squad out front.

Cocking back his pistol, one of the men hopped up and boldly bolted out the door, busting.

Planted in the middle of the street, clutching a 100-round Draco, Kavoni opened fire and filled the man's torso with more holes than a PGA tour.

Moments later, the others emerged from the house, holding their arms up in surrender. Displaying no mercy, Kavoni and Puma littered the pavement with additional shell casings.

His timing precise, King pulled up to the intersection of 7 Mile and Westphalia. As Puma and Kavoni took several steps in the van's direction, their attention was nabbed by a noise behind them.

Clad in only undergarments, a brown-skinned female had crawled out the front door of the burning house. Having stayed inside as long as possible, it sounded as if she was coughing up a lung.

"Have King pull around here," Kavoni instructed before turning to march back toward the house.

The girl looked up to see him closing in. Knowing she was a loose end on the verge of being tied up, fear enabled her to get to her feet and run.

Kavoni casually raised the rifle with one hand and sprayed in a sweeping motion. Shrieking in pain, the girl fell face forward as .223's nearly severed both legs.

As he bore down on the injured girl, who was painfully crawling along the pavement, Kavoni's attentive eyes traveled from an older iPhone lying several feet away to the tourniquet tied around her right arm, something that heroin addicts use for the enlargement of their veins. This explained her being scantily clothed. She'd been inside the house soliciting her young body for drugs.

The Charger sped up alongside Kavoni and Puma lowered her window. "Brah, let's go!"

"Please, don't kill me," the girl softly pled into the pavement.

"I can't kill what's already dead," Kavoni coldly replied before firing two shots into the back of her skull.

Regardless of their age or gender, Kavoni likened a live witness to a liability - something in which a true killer would never invest. So without a morsel of remorse, he hurried to the car and dove into its backseat.

Smashing the gas, King made a right at the corner and headed for the interstate.

With the initial part of their mission complete, it was now time to prepare for the next act.

Fumiya Payne

Chapter 2

In a suburban section of the city called Macomb, a made-up Puma approached the front door of a three-story house and rang its doorbell. Wearing a peach sundress over open-toe sandals, she had a leather handbag attached to her right hand.

"Who is it?" barked a male's voice from behind the door.

"Hi, my name is Amber and I'm one of Jehovah's Witnesses," Puma cheerfully replied.

Gripping a chrome handgun as he peered through the peephole, the shirtless man was intrigued by her silky hair and doll-like features, so much that he shielded the weapon behind his right leg and cracked the door open for a closer inspection.

Puma blushed at the sight of his heavily-tattooed chest, but quickly recovered. "G-G-Good morning, sir," she purposely stuttered while removing a Bible from her bag. "But I was hoping to read you a few scriptures and provide you with one of our magazines that offers hope in this ungodly world."

Lustfully eyeing the outline of her curves beneath the thin dress, he briefly scanned the area before asking if she was alone.

"Not really," she answered with a naive expression. "With this being part of my congregation's territory, there's others on the next block."

"Well, listen, I ain't too comfortable standing at the door like this. But if you willing to come in, then I'm willing to hear more about that magazine."

He noticed her look of uncertainty and thirstily inserted, "I swear I ain't no bad person, Amber. And to be honest, I could really use some spiritual uplifting."

Slyly placing the gun in the drawer of a small table, he unlocked the screen door and pushed it open. "Come on in."

"I can't stay long," she said, timidly stepping into the front room.

Ooh wee! He smiled to himself while closing and locking the front door. *I'm 'bout to fuck the shit out this li'l pretty bitch!*

Upon turning around, his eyes widened right before Puma tased him with enough volts to put down a wild animal. As his stiffened body collapsed onto the carpeted floor, saliva trickled from the corners of his partially-opened mouth. Helplessly watching as Puma slid her hands into latex gloves, the man was appalled by how easily her energy had converted from angelic to devilish. As if reading his thoughts, Puma slipped him a wink before she opened the table's drawer and removed his gun.

After subduing him with zip ties and covering his mouth with a strip of duct tape, she used a prepaid cell phone to send a one-word text: READY.

Accessing the garage through the kitchen, Puma fingered a button on the wall to raise its door. Seconds later, a Dodge Ram rolled inside. As the garage door was lowering, Kavoni and King emerged from the truck in tan Dickies and work boots. Grabbing two duffel bags and a toolbox from the Ram's bed, they followed Puma inside the house.

After having the man brought into the living room, Kavoni opened the toolbox and removed a .22 Smith & Wesson, the suppressor from an AR-15 and a fitted adapter. First picking up the firearm, Kavoni retracted its slide far enough to expose the barrel's threading and unscrewed a small cap. Replacing it with the adapter, he screwed on the suppressor, then racked a round into the gun's chamber. He could now fire suppressed shots that would sound no louder than a child's cough.

Kavoni approached the man and touched the suppressor to his left kneecap. "Where that shit at?"

He shook his head in a clueless manner and Kavoni fired.

His eyes closing in agony, the man released a series of muffled screams.

Known to the streets as Chewy, the man was guilty of running off on a Mexican drug connect for ten bricks of heroin. Strengthened by a slew of savages, he'd been certain his dishonorable deed would go unpunished.

Kavoni placed the gun to his opposite knee and repeated, "Where that shit at?"

Chewy continued feigning ignorance and Kavoni again fired.

After another round of smothered squeals, Kavoni leveled the gun with his crotch. "This the last time I'm asking."

On account of his assailants being barefaced, Chewy knew he was living on borrowed time. So refusing to let them rob him of both his health *and* wealth, he angrily mumbled an indistinct statement.

Kavoni removed the tape. "I couldn't hear you?"

Coldly returning Kavoni's stare, he repeated, "I said, good luck finding it, bitch-ass nigga!"

Kavoni smirked at his bravado, then savagely struck him with the butt of his gun.

When Chewy awakened, he was tied facedown to his kitchen table. Aside from his socks, every stitch of his clothing had been removed.

Capable of moving only his head, he looked left and locked eyes with Puma.

"Welcome back." She smiled, hopping down from the countertop.

Chewy frowned in confusion as Puma slipped out of her sandals and sundress. In Polo briefs and a sports bra, she then gathered her hair in a ponytail and banded it together with a zip tie.

"Nigga, that shit was driving me *insane!*" she said aloud while reaching inside her handbag.

What she removed caused Chewy's heart to skip several beats.

"Aw, you ain't know?" Puma grinned as she equipped herself with a large strap-on that matched her skin complexion. "I like what you like."

When she scooped a glob of Vaseline from a small jar and began lubing up the lambskin penis, Chewy struggled to the point of nearly dislocating his limbs.

"Your thirsty ass thought you was gon' get me up in here and fuck me," she sneered while climbing onto the table. "Not knowing, Puma do all the fucking!"

From in the next room, Kavoni and King could hear Chewy's muffled wails. While this was not a method they would normally adopt, in this instance, his rebellion required a barbaric reward.

The kitchen suddenly grew quiet.

Seconds later, Puma appeared in the doorway, wearing the glistening strap-on and a look of disappointment. "Man, buddy broke down before I could even get the head in."

When Chewy revealed the location of his treasury, they then understand why he wished them good luck in finding it, for it was in a place where no burglar alive would've thought to check.

After retrieving a ladder from inside the garage, Kavoni and King headed out to the backyard - where they aligned the ladder with the roof and carefully climbed up its metal rungs.

Posing as inspectors, they examined various parts of the roof before casually making their way towards the chimney.

Kavoni removed a flashlight from the toolbox and shone it into the darkened enclosure until he noticed the thin cord that was looped around a nail-like object. Handing King the flashlight, he grabbed ahold of the cord and pulled up the heftiness of a black trash bag. When they reentered the house, Puma was then wearing a tracksuit and white sneakers.

Holding their breath in suspense as Kavoni untied the bag, they peered inside and flashed smiles brighter than kids on Christmas. Along with the ten kilos of heroin were bundles of rubber-banded money.

"Y'all might wanna go wait in the car," Kavoni advised them as he removed several items from his duffel bag. "Because shit 'bout to get real messy."

Chewy's fearful eyes were fixed on Kavoni as he slipped into a plastic raincoat.

As King headed out to the garage, Puma hopped up on the countertop and folded her arms.

Kavoni looked over his shoulder, "What's up, you staying?"

Puma smacked her lips. "Come on, nigga, you already know I'm trying to watch this li'l shit."

He flashed an amused smirk as he picked up a large hatchet. Her fascination with violence reminded Kavoni of how they initially became a team…

Fumiya Payne

Chapter 3
10 years ago...

"Gimme the money, muthafucka!"

Decked out in all black with a T-shirt tied over his face, young Kavoni had a large pistol pointed at the face of an Arab store owner. Also present was nine-year-old King, who was planted by the entrance, playing the role of a look-out.

"Just calm down," the Arab said as he slowly lowered his right hand. "The money is yours." Bypassing the register, he instead reached for a loaded .357 Magnum.

Blessed with impeccable reflexes, Kavoni fired twice before he could fully raise the revolver. Hurtling the counter as the Arab collapsed onto the floor, Kavoni kicked the gun from within his reach and turned to the register. Confusedly faced with an abundance of buttons, he spun toward the man for instructions on its opening.

"How the fu——"

Blood poured from a hole in his head and the owner's lifeless eyes stared toward the ceiling.

Seized with panic at his sudden dilemma, Kavoni sensed a movement from behind and pivoted with the gun extended.

It was the owner's nephew, whose mouth hung open in utter shock.

"Open the fucking register!" Kavoni barked, "Before you join him."

After he nervously complied, Kavoni ordered him to kneel on the floor and close his eyes.

"Please," he tearfully pled.

"I said get on the fucking ground!"

Slowly sinking to his knees, the boy began fervently praying in a foreign tongue.

After clearing the register, Kavoni warned the boy not to move, then hopped over the counter.

Forcing himself to remain calm as he and King exited the store, Kavoni's worse fears came to life when a squad car entered the parking lot.

"Just keep walking," he whispered to King as his heartbeat threatened to burst from within his chest.

When one of the officers ordered them to stop and show their hands, it was as if Kavoni's world converted into slow motion. With only a split second to make a decision, he took a deep breath before turning to open fire. His sole intention to give them a headstart, Kavoni purposely missed and yelled for King to run.

Scaling fences and gates as they sprinted through backyards and alleyways, Kavoni could run so fast on account of his little brother. As they hopped a fence behind an apartment complex, King landed wrong and fell to the ground.

"Ahhh!" he cried out in pain while holding his sprained ankle.

Rushing to his brother's aid, Kavoni reached down to assist him. "Bro, you gotta get up," he said in an urgent tone.

King attempted to stand, but the pressure placed on his injured ankle produced an unbearable pain. "I can't, bro," he grimaced.

Slightly bending, Kavoni instructed for King to place his arm around his neck, then hurriedly helped him along. Although he undoubtedly faced a life sentence, Kavoni would prefer to be captured than to abandon his baby brother.

Amid the whirring of an overhead chopper and nearby sirens, they duck off inside one of the apartment buildings.

"We ain't ran far enough," Kavoni mumbled to himself as King tiredly lowered himself to the floor. With a dead store owner and shots fired at officers, he knew authorities wouldn't leave a stone unturned in their search for the suspects.

As he contemplated his next move, Kavoni happened to peek out the building's door and saw several cop cars entering the complex.

"Fuck!" he cursed beneath his breath.

When he turned to look back at King, who was watching him through wide eyes, Kavoni involuntarily teared up.

At only fifteen years old, Kavoni was the caretaker of his little brother. Sometimes forced to sleep inside abandoned houses, he did whatever it took to provide King with food and clothing. But after tonight's events, his usually intrepid heart was plagued with pure fear. He knew that his capture would result in King being placed in foster care, something he once vowed to never allow.

Knowing their time together was limited, Kavoni quickly reached down inside his sweatshirt.

"Here," he said, pressing the robbery money into King's palm. "Hide this in your underwear and don't tell a soul. And if we get split up, don't ever let nobody mistreat you, King. Always choose death over disrespect, you hear me?"

As he slowly nodded, an apartment door opened and a light-skinned girl with box braids poked her head out. She locked eyes with Kavoni and the desperation of his stare tugged at her teenage heart.

"Y'all better hurry up," she warned, opening the door wider in invitation.

Kavoni helped King to his feet and they scurried into the apartment, where neither was prepared for the sight before them.

Slouched on a ragged couch were several hollow-faced addicts who appeared to be among the dead. And lying on an ancient coffee table were syringes, tourniquets, and a host of other accessories associated with the use of heroin.

As they walked past, one of the addicts cracked open a yellowish eye. "Who you done let up in my house, Puma?"

"Some friends from school," she lied, leading them down a short hallway.

Entering a small, neatly-kept room, the girl closed the door behind them and secured it with a butter knife.

Kavoni instantly went over to the curtained window and peeked out, where the area was crawling with law enforcement. He quickly stepped back as the flicker of a flashlight passed over him.

"I'm Puma," the girl said in introduction. "What's y'all names?"

When Kavoni didn't respond, King volunteered the information.

Kavoni pinned him with a scolding stare, to which King innocently shrugged his shoulders.

As Puma was on the verge of asking what part of the city they were from, there was a loud knock at the apartment's front door.

Kavoni mechanically drew his weapon, which Puma eyed with an awed expression.

The incessant knocking snapped Puma out of her trance.

"I'll be right back, she said before reaching to remove the knife from her doorframe. She looked back to catch Kavoni watching her with a skeptical expression. "Nigga, I could've left you out in the hallway," Puma hissed. "So don't dare look at me like I'm no fucking rat!"

Having scrambled into her bedroom, Puma's mother was nervously peeking out its door as she marched past. "Girl, who the fuck you done brought up in here?"

Not bothering to respond, Puma continued marching toward the front door and snatched it open.

"Why the fuck is you banging on my shit like that?" she demanded of the male officer. "Don't you know I gotta take a test tomorrow? My mama ain't here to fix shit to eat. She ain't washed, so I don't know what the fuck I'ma w——"

"Ma'am, ma'am," the officer interrupted as he raised a hand for her to pause. "I'm sorry for your troubles, but we're searching for two suspects wanted in connection with a deadly robbery. And I just need to know if you've seen or heard anything."

"Nah, I ain't saw nothing," Puma lied with a direct stare, "But then again, I ain't been looking, either."

"Well, ma'am, these men should be considered armed and extremely dangerous. So if you see or hear anything, don't hesitate to call 911."

"And if you see my mama, don't hesitate to send her skinny ass home!" Puma said before slamming the door.

Pleased by her performance, she proudly went to inform Kavoni that everything was kosher.

As they were quietly sitting around, Puma took notice of King's injury and inspected the swollen ankle before leaving the room.

"Here," she said, returning with a bag of frozen vegetables. "Put this on there."

While still on his feet - and periodically peering out the window - Kavoni secretly observed Puma's masculine swag and the relative ease with which it was exhibited. But regardless of her sexual preferences, he could only be deeply grateful for who she was internally.

Puma caught him studying her and he quickly averted his eyes.

"So where y'all from?" Puma asked as she turned her attention back to King.

He looked to Kavoni, whose gaze was trained on the carpeted floor.

"King, where y'all from?" Puma persisted.

He hesitated before quietly answering, "Nowhere."

"Nowhere?"

He shook his head in sadness.

"Y'all don't got nowhere to live?" she inquired in disbelief.

He again shook his head.

"What about your parents?"

King looked down before mumbling, "We ain't got none."

Damn! Puma thought to herself. While her living conditions would be intolerable for most, she couldn't imagine being homeless at such a young age.

"You want to watch TV?" she asked King in an attempt to lighten the mood.

A luxury he wasn't often afforded, he eagerly nodded.

As she scanned through her limited channels, a Breaking News update was being aired on Fox.

"I'm currently standing outside of Stop-N-Go carryout, where the owner was gunned down during a brazen robbery by two suspects in dark clothing and T-shirts tied over their faces."

The TV screen switched to the camera recording of Kavoni and King inside the store.

As the reporter went on to cover the story, Puma and Kavoni's eyes were magnetically drawn together. And rather than fear, she regarded him with a look of admiration.

This girl crazy for real, he concluded to himself.

After convincing Kavoni it would be wiser for him and King to stay the night, Puma eventually suggested they become a team. "And you seen me in action. So you already know I don't fold under pressure. And don't forget, I can still be a girl if need be. So trust me, a nigga like me would definitely be beneficial."

And true enough, Puma would prove as beneficial in the past just as much as she did in the present.

Chapter 4
Present day...

On the outskirts of Detroit, a white Range Rover wheeled into a bowling alley and parked in a reserved space at the front of the crowded lot.

Moments later, the interior was illuminated as a woman of foreign descent emerged from its passenger seat. She turned to bark something at the driver before prancing toward the building's entrance with the hem of a Hermes coat hovering near the pavement.

Inside the Range Rover, a bearded Hispanic male sparked a slender cigarette and soothingly inhaled its toxic fumes - a habit for which his wife constantly scolded him. He was midway through the cancer stick when his passenger door opened and a hooded figure gracefully slipped inside.

Quickly recovering from his initial shock, the Hispanic flicked the cigarette at the intruder, thus giving him time to produce a palm-size pistol. "What the FUCK you doing in my car?" he icily inquired while holding the barrel to the intruder's temple.

In answer, a green beam began flickering over the Hispanic's face before it froze between his brows. His attention gained from far away, he clenched his jaw in anger and reluctantly lowered the pistol.

"You got five seconds to tell me what you doing in my car," he growled, "or funeral arrangements will be made for *both* of us."

With a bowling ball bag perched on his lap, Kavoni removed his hood and calmly stated, "I just want a seat at the table."

"What table?" The driver frowned in feigned confusion.

"The same one you let Chewy's disloyal ass eat at."

Displaying no reaction to the name, the driver replied, "I don't know what the hell you're talking about. You obviously have me mistaken for someone else. Now, if you'll excuse me."

Casually unzipping the bowling ball bag, Kavoni removed a large, roundish object and placed it on the dashboard. The Hispanic stared in horror at Chewy's decapitated head.

"Sir, I'm respectfully requesting this nigga's seat," Kavoni said with an expression of raw hunger. "And not to speak ill of the dead, but we both know his head wasn't fit for no crown."

Wrinkling his nose at the vicious stench of the decomposing head, the Hispanic then knew who was responsible for the destruction of Chewy and his top henchmen. During a "breaking news" report, the city had been informed of the heartless house fire massacre and the diabolical discovery of Chewy's headless remains. Unaware if these heinous crimes were connected, officials were urging anyone with information to readily come forward.

"It's my understanding that he ran off with your belongings," Kavoni continued while returning Chewy's head to the bag.

On cue, a Jeep Rubicon pulled alongside the SUV.

Kavoni opened his door to exchange bags with Puma.

"This what he took, plus some," Kavoni informed the Hispanic as he placed the trash bag on the center console. "And should you decide to give me a chance, there's also a number in there where you can reach me at."

He then extended his hand, which the Hispanic hesitantly shook.

"My name's Kavoni, and it was a pleasure meeting you," he said before exiting the vehicle.

As the Rubicon drove off, the Hispanic stared from the bag to the dashboard, still in slight disbelief at what just occurred.

***

Covered in Kevlar while in arm's reach of modified firearms, Kavoni and the others were lying low inside a top floor room at the Ramada Inn.

"I still don't see why you gave him all the money," King grunted in disgust as his thumbs darted over a PlayStation's controller. "'Cause clearly, he sees what type of demo we just put down. So clearly, he knows what's in his best interest."

Speaking in reference to the money given to the Hispanic, King was cursed with a one-track mind - the reason Kavoni suspected he'd never become more than a mere soldier. But in spite of his flawed perspective, Kavoni attempted to correct him.

"King, do you know the full meaning of being a gangster? Because most niggas associate the word with straight violence. And in reality, that's only half of it."

King didn't respond, but his attentive expression encouraged Kavoni to continue. Even Puma's ears had perked up.

"Bro, it ain't no secret that savagery is sometimes significant. But a real gangster will want wisdom to be his boss, and violence just his assistant. Because if a nigga can't think, then regardless of his body count, he gon' have a short story. Whether he's another plot in the cemetery, or an inmate number in the joint."

"And that li'l bread," Kavoni added, "was just a small investment towards an even bigger return."

"I hear what you saying," King stubbornly persisted, "but what if he never calls? Then it's just gon' be a straight loss. That's why I'm saying we should've at least kept the money."

Saddened by the deficiency of his reasoning, Puma lowered her head in shame. It was she who had watched over King when Kavoni went to prison. Puma had done all she could in teaching him. But with their survival the focal point of her life, there had been little time for parenting.

Aware of Puma's internal torment, Kavoni slipped her a subtle headshake before further explaining to King, "Bro, them Mexicans ALWAYS looking for niggas to put on. And when they meet one they feel can be trusted to a certain extent, they'll flood him with TRUCKLOADS of that shit. So trust me, this bitch gon' ring, my baby."

King and Puma were playing the game while Kavoni thoughtfully paced. It was several hours later when the sudden trilling of his phone seized their attention. Kavoni took the call on speaker.

"Come to the door," a voice instructed before abruptly disconnecting the call.

Instantly snatching up a firearm and fanning out, they crouched low and aimed at the door, for *no one* was supposed to know of their location.

After several soundless and suspenseful minutes, Kavoni edged toward the door. He placed an eye to the peephole and peered out at an empty hallway. His heart thumping, he cracked the door open and scanned either side of the hallway before taking in the small duffel bag outside the room across from him. Signaling for Puma and King to provide cover, he grabbed the bag and backpedaled into the room.

As they were huddled around the bed, Kavoni unzipped the bag and they stared at the familiar sight of ten neatly-stacked kilos of heroin. And placed on top was a note, which Kavoni unfolded.

"What it say?" Puma nosily inquired.

Kavoni smiled. "We got thirty days."

By tracking Kavoni down in such a short amount of time, the Hispanic was simply showcasing his reach and resources. So while Kavoni's boldness may have been impressive enough to earn him a seat at the table, it was imperative that he understood how easily he could become what was on the menu.

But because Kavoni was living as if life was a game of chess, his strategic thinking enabled him to see several moves ahead and anticipate his opponent's move. He knew that those who play poorly are checkmated with haste and no remorse. and second chances are as common as honest thieves. So for that reason, he had thought to check into two separate rooms under different names.

After gawking at the scorpion-stamped packages, they quickly returned them to the bag, cleansed the room of fingerprints, and exited the hotel through a back stairwell.

Kavoni was comfortably settled in the backseat of the Rubicon as Puma steered them through traffic. Despite his solemn expression, he was inwardly rejoicing as he gazed out the window. By securing a seat at a table where the food was unlimited, Kavoni was reminded of a promise he'd made on the morning of his release from prison.

Shortly after his nineteenth birthday, Kavoni was arrested for the shooting of a rival gang leader. After sending word to Kavoni that he'd drop the charges only if he was paid ten grand, the shooting victim appeared at every court date upon Kavoni's refusal, thus forcing him to cop out to a five-year sentence. Shipped to one of the most violent prisons in the state, it was there Kavoni would become cellmates with a street legend who'd teach him the importance of placing brain before brawn.

"Men of your caliber have only two options," his cellie, Freddie-D, had told him one night. "It's either fly, or die. And from what I see, you got the ability to soar among the clouds. But you small-minded, my baby. You think enduring the struggle entitles you to a bankroll, and expecting something for nothing ain't even consistent with universal law. When a man steps up to the counter of success, he can't do no *bargaining*. A price must always be paid *up front*, and in *full*."

Never before having the tutelage of a thinker, Kavoni was all ears as Freddie-D continued.

"Trust me, I can sense how badly you want a seat at the table. But you gotta not only be willing to elbow your way to it, but you gotta first figure out how you'll even get inside the room to where the table is. 'Cause a man can't eat what he can't see. And remember, fortune favors the bold, my baby."

On the morning of his release, Kavoni and Freddie-D exchanged a farewell and firm handshake.

"Gratitude for every precious jewel, big homie," Kavoni stated in his sincerest tone. "And I give you my word, until the day my casket drops, I'ma make the streets *salute my savagery!*"

Fumiya Payne

Chapter 5

Without a speck of dust on its gleaming skin, a cranberry-colored Escalade turned off 7-Mile road onto Jo'an Street. Behind the SUV's smoked glass was Kavoni, who clutched the steering wheel in his left hand and a firearm in the other.

As he glided down a street responsible for several dozen homicides a year, Kavoni's attentive eyes scanned his rearview for a tail. While he may have been unafraid of being in an area rarely patrolled by law enforcement, he respected how easily he could become the body beneath another killer's belt.

Slowing before a yellow house where a pair of armed piranhas were posted on the porch, Kavoni drove up on the curb and parked in an adjacent field. With the Ruger on de-cock as he exited the vehicle, Kavoni saluted the two men while approaching a side door to the house, on which he knocked with the butt of his gun.

Moments later, the door was opened by Puma, who had a large Glock wedged in the waistband of her joggers.

"What's good, my baby?" she greeted, stepping aside for him to enter.

"All well," Kavoni replied as he tucked his strap before reaching out to shake her hand.

Following Puma through the trap house, Kavoni paused by the living room to acknowledge King and his best friend, Double-O, who were engrossed in the latest edition of Call of Duty. His complexion the color of motor oil, Double-O had a curly bush of hair and several whiskers of a mustache. However, his innocent image was belied by marble-like eyes that warned of imminent danger.

"What up doe?" Kavoni greeted.

Their eyes never strayed from the TV screen as they returned his greeting with a slight lift of the head. "What up doe?"

Kavoni smirked before he and Puma continued toward the kitchen.

Upon reaching it, Puma grabbed two gas masks with dual breathers and tossed one to Kavoni. Once they had adjusted them over them their faces, she unlocked the door.

When they stepped inside, Kavoni was caught off guard by the scene before him and glanced at Puma.

Shrugging her shoulders, she said in a muffled voice, "It's a new era, my baby,"

Instead of there being women workers in the makeshift drug lab, Puma had delegated the role to three men. But more interestingly, aside from wearing gas masks and latex gloves, she had them working in white jockstraps and Jordan flip-flops.

With their movements being monitored by mounted cameras, Kavoni watched as the trio methodically maneuvered about a large island in the center of the kitchen. Along with kilos of heroin, on the countertop were a number of items he knew to be used in connection with the product being stretched and recompressed.

On account of her familiarity with heroin, Kavoni had appointed Puma over their drug operation. Having been around addicts since infancy, she not only had the necessary experience, but she knew nearly every user on the east side of the city. So while he was aware of King's desire to be in charge, Kavoni was more interested in the accumulation of currency than the accommodation of feelings.

Satisfied at what he witnessed, Kavoni provided Puma with a nod of approval and she led him from the kitchen.

"Bro, we gon' double them bitches up and STILL leave dancing room," Puma excitedly enlightened him as they removed their masks. "So don't worry about nothing. Just sit back and watch me run this bag up."

"Puma, I lost all doubt in you right after we first met," Kavoni said with a sincere expression. "I know exactly what you made of, my baby. My only concern is that we never allow the money to change us. Because we've seen how it's been the ruin of so many friendships. So hold me accountable, as I'll do you the same."

Knowing her best friend was relaying words directly from his heart, Puma matched his energy.

"Bro, you really like the big brother I never had, but always wanted. And I'd love you no less if we was scrapping COPPER for a living. And on top of that," she tapped a finger to her temple, "I keep our purpose right here."

A twinkle of excitement appeared in Kavoni's eyes as he and Puma recited in unison, "We don't fight to eat...we fight to FEED!"

As two friends who shared the ability to exchange substantial thoughts, Puma and Kavoni once concluded that their monstrous ambition required an underlying cause, something far greater than simply coveting riches and its afforded luxuries. So they made a conscious decision to properly provide for their people during their passage through purgatory. And in doing so, they prayed the game-god would allow them to reap the rewards of a balanced scale.

Kavoni was on the verge of leaving when King walked up and asked to have a word with him.

"A'ight, girl," Kavoni said, giving Puma a hug, "I'ma see you in a li'l bit."

"Stay dangerous, my baby," she counseled before turning to head back to the kitchen.

"What's on your mind?" Kavoni inquired as King accompanied him outside.

"I want you to put me in the game, bro. I ain't taking away from Puma, but she ain't the only one who can put up points, my baby."

Knowing this was a conversation that would eventually take place, Kavoni readily responded, "King, have I not been looking after you since your memory can remember?"

He looked away and grumbled, "Come on, bro, you already know the answer to that."

"Well, let me continue to do what I've been doing. And the same amount of food on my plate will be on yours. I just need you to play your position, my baby. Because selling drugs ain't meant for everybody; myself included. It's like boxing, or anything else that requires technique. Either you got it, or you don't. A man gotta know his lane and stay in it, because that's how accidents are avoided." Kavoni placed a hand on King's shoulder. "Bro, I need you to continue watching over Puma. You and Double-O the only ones I trust with her life. So be content with the seating arrangements. But, at the same time, understand that you can eat as much as you want."

King wore a contemplative expression before he finally nodded in appeasement. "A'ight, my baby, I got you."

After gripping King in a brotherly embrace, Kavoni climbed inside the Escalade and placed the strap on his lap. Then, reversing out onto the street, he double tapped horn as he sped off down the block.

En route to Cleveland, Ohio, Kavoni was on the verge of making his initial investment into a sport he enjoyed almost as much as killing.

Chapter 6

Three hours later, Kavoni arrived in a suburban section of Cleveland called Bedford Heights. Turning down the driveway of a beige house, he came upon an older white man who was standing out in the front yard.

"You got here pretty fast," the man commented in a jovial tone as Kavoni exited the truck.

"And I need to return just as quickly," Kavoni curtly replied with a firm handshake.

"Right," the man muttered, slightly offended. "Follow me."

His name was Teddy Bridgewater. The man was a renowned breeder of a vicious bloodline of pitbulls. From three-thousand-dollar stud fees to the selling of Grand Champions, Teddy was highly recommended throughout the underworld circuit of dogfighting.

Kavoni was led to a large fenced-in backyard, where ten kennels were placed in separate rows. Situated over concrete slabs, inside each enclosure was a dog house and two five-gallon buckets that contained dry dog food and water.

A majority of the dogs grew antsy with excitement at the presence of a stranger. While each animal was powerfully built and the derivative of a thorough stud, Kavoni was in search of something that surpassed their fur-coated surface.

After a moment of admiring a Grand Champ named Cowboy, Kavoni locked eyes with a fawn-colored dog who quietly observed him from a far corner of his kennel. As they unblinkingly held each other's stare, Kavoni noticed something that compelled him to step closer.

Curiously taking in the discoloration of the dog's left eye, Kavoni turned to question Teddy in regards to his backstory.

"That there is Squeeze. A eight-month-old male, thirty-six pounds. He got into a li'l scuffle as a pup and lost eyesight in his left eye. He's a good boy, but you can imagine how his condition would cause him to be overlooked."

"Why the name Squeeze?" Kavoni further inquired.

"'Cause that sum-bitch earned it," Teddy said, chuckling at the memory. "Somehow, he had gotten loose and went at it with a much bigger dog. But ol' Squeeze came out on top. When we found him, his left eye was caked in blood, but he still had his jaws locked around the other dog's throat. And mind you, we weren't aware of what happened for TWO HOURS."

Kavoni thoughtfully considered the story before turning back to face the kennel.

While the animal continued to regard him with a close eye, Kavoni took a step closer, bent at the waist and began to speak to him a pitch that was meant for only his ears.

"My name Kavoni, Squeeze. And I've also been the underdog my entire life. So I personally know the feeling. But you know what I've learned?"

Squeeze's head slightly tilted right.

"It's that we are survivors by NATURE. It's what defines us. And all we need is a chance."

Kavoni then squatted before the kennel so that he and the dog were eye level.

"I've finally been given a chance, Squeeze. And if you're willing to join me, I'd like to extend you the same opportunity. But it's up to you, my baby."

As his pondering over the proposal, Squeeze turned his head aside and studied the ground.

Teddy stared in awe when the dog suddenly rose from a seated position and slowly approached the front of his kennel.

Inwardly smiling, Kavoni glanced over his shoulder. "Name your price."

After peeling off $2,500, Kavoni escorted a leash-less Squeeze out to the Escalade - where he opened the passenger door and the dog leaped inside without hesitation.

Climbing behind the wheel, Kavoni brought the engine to life and looked over at Squeeze, who was comfortably settled in his seat.

"I'll never give up on you," he assured the animal before reaching over to caress behind his clipped ear. "And all I ask is that you treat me the same in return."

While it was presently impossible for Kavoni to predict, Squeeze would one day be placed in a position where he'd profoundly display the depth of a dog's devotion.

***

Upon reentering Detroit, Kavoni dropped Squeeze off at home before going to a nearby Walmart to purchase dog food and other household items.

Leaving the store, Kavoni was coming around to the SUVs driver side when he nearly bumped into a woman who was angrily cursing at the flattened back tire of her car.

As he excused himself and attempted to slide past, Kavoni was struck by her strong resemblance to the actor Lauren London. But even more intriguing were her olive-green eyes, which bore a reflection of pain that indicated she was once the recipient of a horrid experience. This being something only a certain caliber of a man could recognize, Kavoni felt compelled to offer his assistance.

"Ma'am, if you got a spare tire, I could literally have you on your way within minutes."

Standing slightly bowlegged in green scrubs and matching crocs, she eyed him with a skeptical expression. "And exactly what would this cost me?" she asked, testing the waters.

"I won't even insult you by saying I'll do it on the strength of how beautiful you are. So a simple 'thank you' would be sufficient enough."

The woman flashed a smile that unveiled a deep dimple in her right cheek. "I think I could manage that."

After Kavoni had replaced the tire with a spare from her trunk, the woman offered him her hand in gratitude. "Thank you so much. I just got off work and you don't know how bad my feet are killing me."

"It was my pleasure," he smiled, reluctant to release her soft, manicured hand. "And by the way, I'm Kavoni."

"I'm Mecca."

"Well, Mecca, I'll let you be on your way. But it would be foolish of me not to ask if we could exchange numbers. Because it's not every day I encounter someone as angelic as yourself."

"That's cute," Mecca smirked. "But, boo, I don't read hood books."

"Hood books?" Kavoni repeated in confusion. "What you mean by that?"

Opening her car door, Mecca answered, "It means…you got the streets written all over you. And I already know how that story ends."

The truth spoken, Mecca slid down into her car and drove off.

Left standing in a state of intrigue, Kavoni inwardly vowed to be more persuasive should they ever again cross paths. *I gotta have her.*

As he stepped up into the Escalade and closed its door, Kavoni was unaware of the ominous eyes watching him from behind the windows of a Ford work van.

Chapter 7

After the completion of their job and a thorough cleansing of the kitchen, Puma rewarded each of the three male workers with $2,000 and a quarter-ounce of the finished product.

"I'ma need y'all again real soon," she said, placing the compressed kilos inside a backpack. "And next time I'ma double the wages."

The four of them were leaving the kitchen when Puma removed the Glock from her waist, gracefully pivoted, and fired two rapid shots. As one of the men collapsed from a set of hollows to his forehead, the other two fearfully jumped back and raised their palms.

"I swear to God I ain't steal nothing!" they uttered in unison.

King and Double-O readily appeared at Puma's side with their guns drawn.

"What the fuck happen?" King inquired as he took in the lifeless form lying in a growing pool of blood.

Ignoring him, Puma pointed her pistol at the two men and issued a promise on which she'd stand with all ten toes of her feet.

"Let this be a warning. Because if I even *think* you mentioned a word of what took place inside this house, I'll hunt you down my motherfucking self. And there ain't a rock you could crawl under."

Vigorously shaking their heads, they swore on the lives of every living family member not to repeat anything even remotely related to today's events.

Puma glared into their enlarged eyes a second longer before lowering her weapon.

"A'ight, get the fuck out of here," she ordered with a nudge of the head. "And stay on standby."

Not once looking back, the two men nearly tripped over their own feet as they hurried from the kitchen.

With the help of King and Double-O, Puma rolled the body inside a blanket and they hauled it outside to a Buick Regal. After stuffing it inside the trunk, Puma instructed the pair from the porch to ditch the car somewhere on the west side.

Retrieving the backpack from the house, Puma joined King and Double-O inside the Rubicon. With enough product to serve the entire east side, it was then a matter of persuading a preferable player to perform beneath new management.

***

Three cars deep, Puma and her team pulled up to the most profitable heroin house once owned by the late Chewy.

As proof that her visit was to simply present a peaceful proposal, Puma alone approached the front door. She raised a gloved hand to knock and heard the unmistakable sound of a round being chambered into the head of a firearm.

"I'm here on business," Puma stated loud enough to be heard. "So you may want to hear me out before you kill your only chance at getting some real money."

Knowing the absence of product was heavily affecting their pockets, Puma was almost certain that curiosity would prevail.

"Who the fuck is you?" demanded the gravelly voice of a male.

"I'm Puma," she emphatically informed. "And I ain't discussing business through no fucking door."

Fully aware of the respect attached to her name, Puma was hardly surprised when the door was partially opened.

Boldly entering the house, the first thing she noticed were three gunmen who were posted at various points, with their index fingers hovering over the triggers of mini assault rifles.

These li'l niggas standing on it, she approvingly admitted to herself with a subtle smirk.

"So what's up?" questioned the gravelly voice, which belonged to a 24-year-old known as Dolphin. Although he, too, had a handgun held down at his side, his suave demeanor suggested he was the hustler of his circle.

"That nigga Chewy taking a dirt nap," Puma blatantly announced. "Which means that water supply is cut off. But I'm saying..." She locked eyes with Dolphin, "If you looking for a better source, then you can deal directly with me. And this well ain't drying up."

Not one to miss a beat, Dolphin inquired, "And what makes you a better source?"

"Because I won't have you living in a low-ceiling house. You can grow as big as your ambition allows."

Undoubtedly missing out on thousands a day, Puma could sense the internal confliction in which Dolphin was weighing his options. He could either stay and likely starve in a familiar land, or take a risk and relocate his pack to a foreign territory.

"What this spot do on a good day?" Puma asked, interrupting his thoughts.

"Like, ten bands," Dolphin proudly answered.

"And I'm assuming dog had you on a salary. So what was he giving you on a weekly basis?"

Shocked by the precision of her prediction, Dolphin humbly responded, "Five thousand."

Puma openly scoffed at the indecency of his pay.

"Here's what I'll do," she offered. "I'll front you the first load on consignment. Then you can use your profits to re-up. But you don't shop with nobody but me."

Thinking this was too good to be true, Dolphin asked, "And you saying I can cop as much as I want?"

Puma nodded. "But only under one condition."

"And what's that?"

"First, I'ma need you to convince the workers from the other spot on Whittier to fall in line. Then, once you got both houses cranking, I want you to open up a third one. But it'll be your job to govern all three, and I'ma just be the one supplying you with the 'work'."

This bitch can't be serious, Dolphin thought to himself in disbelief. How often did one go from being an underfed underboss, to a patriarch at the pyramid's pinnacle? But as doubt was quickly overridden by desire, Dolphin asked Puma if she knew the amount of heroin required to operate three houses.

In answer, Puma made a phone call and instructed the person on the other end to drop off her brother. A minute later, they heard footsteps ascend the porch, followed by a soft thud. Fetching the backpack, Puma tossed it before Dolphin's feet.

"That's two bricks, and I want fifty off each one. I only danced on it once, so there's plenty of room for a two-step. But keep in mind, the more fire it is, the faster it'll go. And turnover rate is crucial when you got a steady supply."

Because this was an opportunity too beneficial to bypass, Dolphin assured Puma that failure was not an option. "It's fourth-and-goal, my baby. And by all means will I get in that end-zone."

Before leaving, Puma paused at the front door and turned to piercingly stare into Dolphin's eyes.

"I can respect a hog's hunger and accept a student's mistake. But the deceit of a SNAKE..." Puma shook her head disapprovingly. "That's something I won't tolerate." With that said, Puma saluted in closure, then spun on her heels and exited the house.

Climbing back inside the Rubicon, she motioned for King to drive.

"So what you think?" he asked as the three-car convoy slithered off into the night.

Puma smiled. "I think we gon' need a small army if them li'l niggas fuck that bag up. 'Cause they toting big shit."

While Puma could've easily created her crew's own clientele, she convinced Kavoni it was wiser to go with what was already in motion. Because not only was it time efficient, but it required minimal involvement and maximum profits.

And in regards to the dangers of dealing with wild dogs, her philosophy was simple: what's a pack of wolves to a family of grizzlies?

Chapter 8
Later that night...

On I-75, King pulled the Rubicon behind a Chrysler 300 that was stalled on side of the highway with its hazard lights flashing. A second later, two women emerged from the broken-down car, carrying large handbags. Both equally attractive, one had a pecan complexion, whereas the other was the color of chocolate.

Puma wore a slight scowl as they approached the Jeep.

Jazz, the pecan-complected woman, opened the back door opposite of Puma and explained, "I know I didn't mention it over the phone, but this my girl who just started working with me, and I was wondering if we could give her a ride."

Clearly I ain't gon' leave the bitch out here on side of the road, Puma thought to herself. But rather than voice a sarcastic response, she nudged her head in invitation.

Once the two women were settled inside the jeep, Jazz leaned over to kiss Puma's cheek. With her hair worn in royal blue faux locks, she owned a curvaceous frame that came free of charge.

"Thank you," she whispered into Puma's ear, then introduced everyone to her friend, Unique.

King turned in his seat, "That's your real name?"

"According to my birth certificate." She smiled.

"Well, I'm King," he said, returning her smile, "And this my man, Double-O."

After slipping Double-O a nod of acknowledgment, it was Unique's turn to question King in regards to the authenticity of his name.

"My real name Kingdom," he verified, "but everybody call me King for short."

"Wow, that's different," Unique said, genuinely impressed.

As he merged back into traffic, King cockily replied, "That's 'cause I'm a different type of nigga."

Dropping Unique off first, they arrived at an apartment complex in southwest Detroit. Drawn to her flawless figure and Barbie-like beauty, King exited the Jeep along with her.

"Look, I ain't even gon' hold you up," he said, placing his back against the Jeep. "But I'm saying, though, I wanna get to know you. I think you beautiful, and I'm just tryna see if you got the personality to match."

"Listen to you," Unique smirked. "Trying to be all smooth and shit."

"Nah, I'm just being me, yo. Like I said earlier, I'm different from the average."

"Let me keep it a buck with you, li'l buddy," she sassily replied. "I'm a lot to deal with. Like yourself, I'm also different. Which means I don't tolerate the shit some of these basic bitches do. So if a nigga ain't coming correct, then he can bypass me with the bullshit. *Period.*"

"And I can respect that. But I'm saying, if you think I'm a fraud..." King nodded his head at the Jeep. "Then just ask your girl Jazz about me. 'Cause she know what I'm on, you feel me?"

Unique eyed him for a minute before finally nodding in compliance.

"A'ight, I'ma give you a shot. But you only getting one. So you better not miss."

Climbing back inside the Jeep, King was all smiles as he shifted it into drive and sped out of the complex.

***

"Oh my God, daddy, I can feel that dick in my CHEST!" Jazz screamed as her ankles were pinned to either side of her head.

Hovering over her in a sports bra and briefs, Puma was forcefully filling her womb with all ten inches of her curved strap-on.

"Why you stopping?" Jazz angrily protested when Puma abruptly pulled out. "I was just about to——"

Puma stifled her statement with a passionate kiss.

"Mmmm," Jazz moaned at the expert tangle of Puma's tongue.

Breaking the kiss, Puma slowly trailed her lips down Jazz's satiny skin until reaching the throbbing clitoris that peeked from between fattened lips. As if a paintbrush, she used her tongue to manipulate the small organ with long, sensual strokes.

With one hand gripping Puma's head and other clawing at the sheets, Jazz's eyes rolled upwards before she released the high-pitched scream of an opera singer.

After swallowing every spurt of the syrupy substance, Puma kissed her way back up to Jazz's mouth and offered her some of the sweet remnants.

Once they had showered and eaten, the two lovers climbed back in bed and watched a movie on Netflix.

"Baby, can I ask you something?" Jazz asked as her head was lying on Puma's tattooed chest.

"Anything, girl."

Jazz raised up to look Puma in the eyes. "How come you've never let me get you off? I mean, I've never even seen you completely naked before. Is it because I don't turn you on like that, or something?"

Puma looked away before shaking her head. "Nah, that ain't got nothing to do with it."

Laying an affectionate hand on Puma's cheek, Jazz persisted in a pleading tone, "Then what is it, baby?"

Puma moved to get up and Jazz grabbed ahold of her arm. "Where you going?"

"Man, watch out," Puma said, snatching away. "I ain't about to do this shit with you right now."

As Puma got dressed and left the room, Jazz was left behind with a puzzled expression and the feeling of rejection.

Why won't she trust me? she thought to herself in frustration.

Their relationship dating back nearly seven months, Jazz had proven her loyalty to Puma by placing herself in a position to infiltrate Chewy's criminal enterprise. Using her sexuality as a means of gathering intel that would assist in his dethronement, Jazz had faithfully reported every spilled secret back to Puma. Unremorseful of her actions, she only wished that Puma would return the loyalty by granting her access inside the room in which her pain was hidden.

Hunched over a workbench in the basement, Puma wore a concentrated look as she handled the handgun used in connection with the murder she committed earlier that day. Her hands moving with a practiced efficiency, she swiftly performed the several steps required in disassembling the gun.

Upon removal of the slide, she pinched a spring beneath it that released the barrel. Replacing it with one that had a different thread count, the gun was now like brand new. While most people would simply dispose of the murder weapon, Puma shared a sinister bond with the Glock she referred to as "Martha".

Before leaving the basement, Puma picked up a small chisel and carefully engraved a nick onto the gun's slide. That being a symbol of her body-count, on the side of Martha were now a total of four nicks.

Chapter 9

"What up, doe?" Puma greeted upon answering her phone. Donning a pair of dark shades and a fitted ballcap, she was slouched in the passenger seat of a purple Hellcat. And occupying her lap was her over-protective partner, Martha.

"A'ight, meet me on Linwood," Puma instructed after briefly listening to the caller. "I'll be there in like ten minutes."

No sooner than the call was disconnected, her phone again vibrated. The ensuing conversation being identical to the first, this had been a continuous cycle since earlier this morning.

Immediately after orchestrating the operation of three drug houses, Puma offered an army of addicts free samples along with her phone number. Assuring them that they'd receive the same potent product upon every purchase, there was soon a ceaseless ringing of her phone. But because she regarded herself as a Boss, hand-to-hand transactions would be short-lived. Once the phone was earning a steady $5,000 per day, she'd pass the baton to one of her promising pups.

To prevent excessive driving, Puma would instruct a number of callers to park on a particular street. Then, after a quick exchange with the line of cars, she'd direct the next wave of callers to a different location. That not only kept her constantly moving, but enabled her to service multiple people at once.

While sipping from a bottled water, Puma glanced over at Jazz as she steered them toward their destination. Since the incident that occurred the other night, she could feel the distance between them slowly expanding. And Jazz simply knew way too many secrets.

"It ain't no mystery that I like you," Puma said, laying a hand on Jazz's thigh. "But if you ain't got the patience to see how we gon' unfold, then I understand, my baby. 'Cause I know I got issues."

"It's not even about patience, Puma," Jazz replied without removing her eyes from the road. "Sometimes I just wonder if I'm planting rocks."

"Planting rocks?" Puma frowned. "Why you say that?"

To avoid an argument, Jazz shook her head. "Don't even worry about it, Puma. I'ma just keep playing my position until you decide to bench me."

"Nah, tell me why you said that," Puma insisted.

Jazz sighed loudly. "Because I'm wondering if I'm wasting my fucking time, Puma. Like, if I'm planting my heart in unfertile grounds. 'Cause sometimes you make me think this shit gon' blossom into thorns instead of roses. So it's like, I love you, but I gotta be cautious as the same time. And that shit gets frustrating as fuck."

Struck by the profoundness of her statement, Puma was pondering over a proper response, when Jazz turned onto Linwood, where a number of cars were idling in wait.

"We ain't done with this," Puma said as she systematically slid Martha in her waistband, then grabbed a backpack from between her legs and exited the car. While Jazz circled the block, she'd go from car-to-car and handle the exchanges.

Filled with drugs and money, the backpack was used as a safety precaution. Whether she was on foot or inside the car, Puma could easily slip it over her shoulders and evade law enforcement. And with the speed of a greyhound, her capture was unlikely.

As Puma approached the last car, she leaned down on its passenger side. "What you need, love?"

Although the woman's mouth begun moving, Puma was unable to hear a single syllable, for time had frozen at the sight of the person behind the wheel. Were it not for the tint of her frames, there would have certainly been a mutual recognition.

Reclaiming her composure, Puma quickly eyed the bills given to her and dropped several baggies into the woman's palm.

Her timing perfect, Jazz pulled up and Puma hurried around to the car and hopped in.

"Please don't question me," Puma said in a hurried tone as she closed the door, "But I need you to turn on the next street and park."

Jazz could hear the urgency in her voice and wordlessly complied.

"Here, take this," Puma said as she handed Jazz the backpack and literally pushed her out of the car.

"Be careful, baby," Jazz said as Puma quickly climbed over the console.

"You ain't seen me today," Puma forewarned her before closing the door and peeling off.

Pulling up to an intersection, Puma scanned both ways before she spotted the Honda idling at a red light.

Carefully staying several cars back, she followed the couple to an impoverished neighborhood on the west side.

Puma passed the car as it turned into the driveway of a small house. Parking down the street, she stared in her side mirror as the male driver exited the Honda and accompanied the woman inside the house.

Puma was trembling with rage as a set of tears slowly trailed along her smooth cheeks. Removing her glasses to angrily wipe at her face, she reached for Martha and forcibly fed a hollow-point into her chamber. It was time to seize the retributive moment for which she'd been anxiously awaiting.

As she reached for the door handle, Puma suddenly recalled the counsel Kavoni had once given her.

"If your life ain't on the line, never react without first mapping it out. Because something carefully-planned can possibly prevent you from catching a life sentence. And I need you out here with me, my baby. So don't ever crash out unless you absolutely have to."

Reluctantly adhering to the wisdom of her best friend's words, Puma released the door handle.

"But I'ma see you soon, muthafucka," she inwardly vowed while driving away.

Fumiya Payne

Chapter 10

Behind the tinted windows of a rental, a watchful Kavoni was parked down the street from one of his heroin houses. Attentively seated beside him was Squeeze, who also stared in the same direction.

After a week of listening to Puma boast on the high volume of traffic, Kavoni wanted to witness it firsthand. And true enough, there was a never-ending appearance of addicts who were arriving by way of wheels and feet.

Kavoni was on the verge of pulling off when a growling Cutlass "442" came barreling down the block. Its brake lights flashed as it loudly skidded to a stop and parked across the street from the green house. On account of its shiny exterior and gigantic gold wheels, Kavoni was curious to see who emerged from the car.

Accompanied by a shapely-built woman and his friend, Double-O, it was King who drunkenly unfolded himself from the driver seat of the candy-painted Cutlass.

This li'l nigga don't listen, Kavoni fumed to himself as King led the way inside a house in which he was strictly forbidden.

Kavoni waited several minutes before exiting the sedan. This was an error he would not excuse.

Approaching the house, Kavoni performed a signature knock and was soon let in by a hooded hooligan holding a high-powered handgun.

"What's good, my baby?" Dolphin greeted as he rose from a couch to shake hands with Kavoni.

"What's good?" Kavoni replied before glaring at Double-O, who guiltily averted his gaze.

Before inquiring about King's whereabouts, Kavoni took a moment to briefly study the setup inside the house. Along with the gunman that opened the door, two more were present, also armed with fully automatics. Then directly beside a wooden coffee table, which was littered with heroin-filled baggies, was a large bucket of acid. This, he knew, was for the disposal of drugs should the house get raided.

Everyone's attention was seized by a sudden rap at the door.

Dolphin studied the screen of an iPad, where a camera feed showed a lone figure standing on the porch. A nudge of his head sent a teenage boy scurrying toward the door.

"What you need?" he questioned through the mailbox slot.

"Gimme two grams," a male's voice answered before slipping two hundred-dollar bills into the slot.

In the midst of their transaction, the sensual wails of a woman began bellowing from above.

Marching upstairs two steps at a time, Kavoni came upon a closed bedroom door and opened it.

Met with the barrel of King's gun, Kavoni's eyes blazed with anger at the sight of his brother standing behind the exposed bottom of his female companion.

"Damn, my baby," King slurred as he lowered his weapon, "I almost shot the shit out yo' ass!" Except for the jeans that were pooled around his ankles, the fornicator was fully clothed.

"Pull your shit up and let's go."

"Come on, bro, let me——"

"This ain't no motherfucking hotel, King. The feds can run up in this bitch at any given minute. That's why I told you to stay the fuck away from here. Now get your shit together and let's go!"

With his window down, Kavoni was double parked beside the Cutlass when King exited the house.

"Get in," he ordered him.

After telling Double-O to drop the woman off, King said he'd see them in the morning, then joined Kavoni inside the Lincoln.

"Brah, don't be mad at me," King grinned after closing the door. "You know I didn't mean no harm."

"Cut the games, bro. We both know you was trying to show off for that li'l girl."

Aside from lacking the wisdom of a seasoned criminal, King longed for a woman's praise and approval - a weakness of which Kavoni was fully aware.

In spite of King being his beloved brother, Kavoni would not turn a blind eye to his defective behavior because it could not only directly affect him, but subject the entire team to the consequences of his costly mistakes. So as the elder and more sensible sibling, it was his duty to privately reprove him for deeds deemed inappropriate. Kavoni just hoped that he could reach him before he was forced to revoke his place at the table.

Fumiya Payne

Chapter 11
Thirty days later...

With a duffel bag perched on his passenger seat, Kavoni turned into the lot of a car dealership in Dearborn, Michigan and parked near its front entrance.

Met by a female employee, Kavoni was instructed to leave the bag in the car, then led inside the building and shown to the manager's office.

"Good afternoon," greeted a well-dressed Hispanic, who stood beside a large desk. Aside from being the manager, he was a close relative of the man responsible for Kavoni's newfound wealth.

The manager stepped past Kavoni and closed the door. Placing a finger to his lips, he then produced a small wand and motioned for Kavoni to raise his arms. After slowly running the wand over Kavoni's clothing, the manager offered him a seat and stated, "Just a safety precaution."

Kavoni shrugged in indifference. "I have nothing to hide."

"So, Mr. McClain," the manager said as he settled himself in the leather seat behind his desk. "I'm assuming business went well."

"Indeed."

"And do you foresee any difficulty in repeating the process?"

"Not at all," he answered with a steady gaze.

The manager leaned forward to shorten the distance between he and Kavoni. "Sir, you must understand that this monthly arrangement is to continue for an indefinite amount of time. With only two exceptions."

Well aware of the exceptions being either death or imprisonment, Kavoni replied, "I've waited a long time for this seat, and I don't plan on giving it up anytime soon."

They were holding one another's stare when the female employee poked her head into the room.

"It's all there," she informed the manager, referring to the $250,000 inside the Nike bag.

Sliding a car key across the desk, the man instructed for Kavoni to follow the woman. "And we'll see you next month, Mr. McClain.

Oh, and by the way," he added, causing Kavoni to pause in the doorway and turn, "We tacked on another ten."

Outside, Kavoni was escorted to a white Bentley GT coupe with navy blue interior.

"Be sure to check the air pressure of your tires when you get a chance," the woman casually stated.

Kavoni tucked himself inside the Bentley's cabin and awakened it with the touch of a button. Topping off at a speed of nearly 200 mph, he understood the reason behind their car selection. In the event he was pulled over, he had an option of taking his chances in court, or utilizing the supercharged engine.

As Kavoni sped out of the dealership, he glanced in his rearview and noticed the purple Hellcat in pursuit. Several lights down, he turned into a Wendy's restaurant and parked.

While Kavoni went inside to use the restroom, Jazz exited the Hellcat and slid behind the wheel of the wing-emblemed coupe. When Kavoni emerged from the restaurant, he bypassed the car and joined Puma in the Hellcat.

"Hi-C, with no ice," he smiled, passing Puma her favorite drink.

"Yo, I swear I'd date you if I did dudes," she joked while shifting into reverse.

Using police scanners, the two cars hopped on I-75 and weaved through traffic as they raced back toward their hometown. In possession of enough drugs to earn them several decades in a federal prison, they were anxious to return to the environment in which they felt the safest.

***

Upon their arrival back in Detroit, they drove to their trap house on Jo'an. Accessing its garage through an alleyway, Puma parked beside it, while the Bentley drove into the small enclosure.

As they exited the car, Kavoni and Puma paid no attention to a black minivan that was sitting in the vacant field. Not until they entered the garage did Jazz emerge from the coupe.

"Thank you, love," Puma said, pecking her lips in gratitude. "Now I need you to go wait for me in the car real quick."

After lowering the garage door, Puma and Kavoni slipped on leather gloves and engaged in a bit of manual labor. They first jacked up the right side of the car and used lug wrenches to simultaneously remove both tires. Then when all four were removed, they relieved them of their air with a decompression hose.

Placing one of the four flattened tires on top of a small machine, Kavoni stepped on its pedal and the rubber was slowly stripped away from the rim as it spun in a circular motion.

Once the tire was completely separated, they could only marvel at the package attached to its inner lining.

Carefully wrapped in saran and gray duct tape were five kilos of heroin.

Kavoni smiled at Puma, "We struggled together..."

She grinningly replied, "Now we gon' *bubble* together!"

With all twenty kilos placed inside her backpack, the two quickly assembled the car back to its original condition. Then, raising the garage door, they stepped out into the alley - with Kavoni clutching a chrome snub nose at his side.

"I'ma be working with Squeeze tomorrow," he said, accompanying Puma to the Hellcat. "But I'm available if you need me."

"I'm good, brodie," Puma assured him as she placed the backpack inside the car. "So just focus on what you doing, and I'll do the rest."

Kavoni smirked in adoration before draping an arm around her.

"Longevity is unlikely without balance, my baby. So no matter how raw I may consider myself, I would only last for so long if it wasn't for you. Because a commander is only as strong as his general."

Highly appreciative of his praise, Puma lowered her head to hide the reddening of her cheeks, which was something only Kavoni was able to accomplish.

After they'd agreed to check in before sunrise, Puma slipped in the passenger seat and the Hellcat pulled off.

The headlights of the minivan suddenly blinked on and it followed behind her. With King at its wheel and Double-O riding shotgun, Kavoni offered a crisp salute as they rolled past.

Reentering the garage, he folded himself inside the coupe and reversed into the alley. As he quickly hopped out to lower the garage door, Kavoni had no idea that his movements were being watched through a set of binoculars.

Chapter 12

At an unoccupied golf course on the city's outskirts, Kavoni was holding a stopwatch as he stood on top of a steep hill. Down below was Squeeze, who attentively eyed him from a seated position. Wearing a weighted dog vest, he panted in slight exhaustion.

Beginning the morning with "road work", which consisted of a two-mile walk, Kavoni allowed the dog some water and a brief break before engaging him in his current exercise. Referred to as chain-pulls, Kavoni preferred the thirty-pound vest over the traditional use of a barbell-attached chain. And for the protection of his paws, he preferred the golf course on account of its smooth surface.

"Go!" Kavoni barked, simultaneously starting the watch.

Squeeze lurched forward and powered up the hill with muscles rippling throughout his fawn-colored frame. Fiercely loyal to that savior up top, his eyes never strayed.

"Nine seconds!" Kavoni praised as he bent down to lovingly pet what had become a piece of his heart. "That's a good BOY, Squeeze!"

After thirty minutes of chain pulls, Kavoni relieved Squeeze of the vest and they walked back to the car. He stooped down along the way to pocket a single golf ball.

Back at home, they went down into the basement to begin the next exercise, which was known as "milling". Whereas the average trainer simply placed his dog on the treadmill for various amounts of time, Kavoni had adopted a more strenuous and strategical technique.

Rinsing off the golf ball, he placed it in Squeeze's mouth and equipped him with a loosened muzzle. That was to not only prevent him from spitting out the ball, but to also force him to control his breathing while running.

"There we go, boy," Kavoni encouraged him as he knelt before the treadmill. "Control our breathing and we control the fight."

To attain the exalted and much sought-after title of "Grand Champion", a dog must acquire five consecutive wins. So, with his first bout scheduled in less than a month, Squeeze would be daily subjected to a rigorous and repetitive training. Incorporating every known trick, Kavoni would ensure that his fighter was fully prepared for their pursuit of prominence.

Removing Squeeze from the treadmill after thirty minutes, Kavoni gave him a bowl of water, which the dog thirstily drank. They then headed out to a fenced-in backyard, where Squeeze was placed inside an aboveground swimming pool. Known as "water work", this was also to build strength and endurance.

After ending the day's exercise with another two-mile walk, they returned home for a bath and dinner. As part of his diet, Squeeze was fed a bowl of high protein dog food, two chicken breasts, and a small portion of fresh spinach - which was for the thickening of his blood. Once he was done eating and taken out for his nightly bowel movement, Kavoni then laid the dog across the bed for a full body massage.

Halfway through the massage, which Squeeze was thoroughly enjoying, Kavoni received a phone call from Puma.

"What's good, my baby?"

"We got a problem…"

Kavoni listened for a moment before replying, "A'ight, say less. I'm on my way."

***

Parked on a backstreet behind one of the city's most notorious housing projects, Puma, Dolphin, and two of his soldiers were standing at attention when a blue sedan rolled up. With its headlights off, the black minivan was idling at the rear of the block. Unfolding himself from sedan's leather interior, Kavoni wore a solemn expression as he approached the group.

"What happened?" he promptly inquired, his focus on Dolphin.

"I was coming inside the spot," one of his soldiers, Taylay, readily informed, "And two niggas popped out and——"

"Was I talking to you?" Kavoni icily interrupted.

"Nah, but I'm saying——"

Taylay's mouth instantly went mute as a chrome Magnum magically appeared in Kavoni's mitt.

"Nigga, you don't say SHIT, unless I address you."

Puma's hand inched toward her waist and lingered near Martha. Having previously warned them of her intolerance for deceit, she'd slaughter all three at the slightest gesture of aggression.

"But since you like talking so fucking much," Kavoni gritted as he aligned the barrel with Taylay's mouth, "Tell me who got my shit."

Taylay was speechless as he peered into the piercing pupils of a proven predator.

"Talk, nigga!" Kavoni barked, thumbing back the hammer.

His eyes rapidly blinking, Taylay stammered, "I – I——"

"Now this nigga can't talk," Kavoni chuckled.

 Bang!

As Taylay was hurled against a car door before lifelessly sliding to the ground, Kavoni lowered the smoking gun and redirected his attention to Dolphin.

"So what happened?"

By now, Martha was in Puma's hand and eager to obey.

Forcibly maintaining his composure, Dolphin explained how, after first checking the camera, he opened the door for Taylay, when three masked gunmen blitzed the living room. "…I ain't never froze up, my baby, but you know it's whoever draw first. And them niggas wasn't fucking around. They even smoked one of my men."

Studying Dolphin's eyes for a trace of dishonesty, Kavoni instinctively decided he was being genuine. However, the man beside him reeked of a foul odor. In a split second, Kavoni had his pistol placed within inches of the man's face. "Tell me what you know, or I'm squeezing."

Quickly raising both hands, he rattled off, "All I know is Taylay said some nigga name Teezy was gon' pay him to let them run up in the spot. But he ain't say nothing about nobody getting kilt."

He lifted his eyebrows and emphatically added, "Bro, on *Granny*, I ain't have nothing to do with this shit."

"But you knew about it," Kavoni condemned him. "Which means your loyalty belonged more to this dead nigga than it did to Dolphin. And he the one that's *feeding* you."

Shamefully lowering his head, he mumbled, "I know, bro. I fucked up."

"Yeah, you did," Dolphin nodded as he eyed one of his most beloved soldiers. "But we gon' figure it out, my baby."

Jerking his head towards Dolphin with a hopeful expression, he hastily inserted, "Anything."

This nigga fried, Kavoni smirked to himself while wedging the weapon back in his waistband.

As the man exhaled a sigh of relief, Kavoni questioned Dolphin in regards to what was taken.

"Like, thirty-six racks and fifteen zips."

Kavoni mentally calculated the loss before shrugging it off; for he knew stickups were part of the game. But so is revenge.

"A'ight, this what we gon' do," he explained to Dolphin. "I want you to shut your spot down. Then tell them niggas in the other two spots to start giving out their phone numbers. 'Cause within a week, we shutting them down, too. It's time to start moving off straight phone action."

"And as far as you," he said in regards to Dolphin's position, "I'ma need you to start moving weight. And set the prices to where niggas *gotta* come shop with you. 'Cause this shit coming in like clockwork."

This sounding like music to Dolphin's ears, he solemnly swore to make Kavoni a rich man. "But you know it's gon' be some niggas who feel like I'm stepping on their toes."

"It don't matter." Kavoni shrugged. "Because we can either step on toes, or step over bodies."

With her hands clasped behind her back, Puma accompanied Kavoni back to his car.

"So what you want me to do?" she quietly questioned in reference to the robbery.

"Nothing yet," he answered, opening his car door. "Because when we spill blood, we gon' make sure it belongs to only those responsible. So for now...just listen. Because the streets definitely gon' talk."

Kavoni was driving down the block, when several gunshots suddenly rang out. Bending the corner, he inwardly commended Dolphin for making the right call in deciding to execute his disloyal soldier.

Fumiya Payne

Chapter 13

The scent of impending death hung heavily in the air.

With Double-O in the back and Puma up front, King was behind the wheel of a SRT Dodge Charger as they followed an older Yukon through the rainy streets of downtown. Wearing hooded tracksuits and tightly-laced sneakers, they were each in possession of a switch-equipped Glock.

In applying Kavoni's advice, it had taken only several days to hear of Teezy boastfully referring to his role in the robbery. And for a reasonable fee, they were able to locate him and his accomplice the following morning as they dropped Teezy's baby mother off at work.

When the Yukon's right-turn signal began blinking, Puma pressed a button to retract the sunroof and Double-O lowered his window. The plan was for King to speed alongside the SUV once they were on a residential street.

Switching the Glock to fully auto, Puma prepared to stand up in her seat, when the SUV turned the corner and suddenly lurched forth in acceleration.

"Go! Go! Go!" she barked at King.

As he punched the gas in pursuit, Puma came out the sunroof, took aim and began firing at the SUV.

One of her shots blew out a back tire, and the slickness of the road caused Teezy to lose control of the wheel and slam into a parked car.

When he jumped out of the driver seat and took off running, Puma swiftly slipped out through the sunroof in pursuit.

Exiting the Charger, King and Double-O were creeping toward the SUV when a hail of gunfire erupted from its passenger side.

As they took cover behind a conversion van, Double-O glanced at King and could see a reflection of fear in his eyes. But he understood, for this was his best friend's first appearance on the front lines.

Double-O peeked around the van, then turned back to King. "Stay right here, my baby."

King grabbed his arm. "Bro, you don't even know where he at."

He grinned in amusement. "Nigga, I'm Double-O."

Boldly stepping out from behind the van, Double-O opened fire while advancing toward the SUV. With two additional clips in tow, he intended to use the ample amount of ammo to his advantage.

While fearfully fleeing from the side of the SUV, the shooter blindly returned fire and managed to strike Double-O in the arm.

Grunting in pain as the limb numbly fell to his side, Double-O emptied the clip in the shooter's direction before crouching behind a pickup truck.

When bullets began banging into the truck's frame and whizzing past his head, Double-O knew he had to act fast. He first ejected the spent cartridge and laid the Glock on his lap. Then, reaching in his pocket to remove a fresh clip, he used his stomach as leverage for its insertion into the gun. But with the use of only one hand, Double-O was now faced with an even bigger dilemma: how to rack a bullet into the gun's chamber.

On pure instinct, Double-O leaned down to peer beneath the truck and saw the shooter sneaking towards him.

The hunter was now being hunted.

In a move of desperation, Double-O placed the top half of the gun between his teeth. Then, closing his eyes, he savagely bit down on the slide and used his mouth to cock the gun back.

Just as a round entered the chamber, the shooter's shadow appeared at the rear of the truck, leaving Double-O with only a split second to raise the gun and fire. As the barrage of bullets blew the shooter backwards, Double-O slouched against the truck and exhaled in relief.

Meanwhile, a relentless Puma was chasing Teezy through backyards and alleyways like U.S. Marshals would a wanted suspect. When he reached for the top of a wooden fence in an effort to hurl himself over, Puma stopped running and carefully aimed for his center mass.

Two well-placed hollows played hide-and-seek near his spine, and Teezy cried out before falling flat on his back. Wearing a pained expression as he rolled onto his side, he looked up at Puma as she closed in. "What the FUCK, yo?"

"You robbed the wrong spot, my baby," Puma replied as she leveled her gun with his head.

"It wasn't my idea," Teezy pleaded as he placed a protective hand before his face.

"Then whose was it?"

"That nigga Musa!"

Puma frowned. "Musa?"

"On my mama, he made us do it," Teezy said, taking in labored breaths. "He said it was some corny niggas from Flint up in there."

While Puma didn't intend on directly involving Kavoni, this was news he'd definitely want to hearing about.

"Musa lied to you," Puma informed Teezy. "So take that up with him when y'all meet up."

After dumping three rounds into the crown of Teezy's head, Puma concealed herself between two houses as she texted King her location.

The Charger pulled up a minute later, and she hurried around to the passenger side and hopped in.

As King sped off, Puma glanced in the backseat.

"Marjuan!" she shrieked in alarm when she saw him slumped over, barely conscious. Puma was so distraught that she was unaware of her addressing Double-O by his government name.

"What the fuck happened?" she barked at King.

"We gotta get him to a hospital," he worriedly answered. "He got hit somewhere in the arm, and he losing blood like a bitch."

"I'ma be a'ight," Double-O weakly assured them, then flashed a smile that revealed his chipped front tooth, which resulted from him biting down on his gun.

Short for 007, in relation to the movie character James Bond, Double-O was given his nickname on account of his creative skillset and action-packed lifestyle. And after his latest stunt, it was safe to say that the nickname was both earned and befitting.

Fumiya Payne

Chapter 14

After serving two years inside a juvenile facility for a drug offense, 18-year-old De'Marco Sanders stood beneath the morning sunlight, anxiously awaiting the opening of the prison's release gate. Wearing a jean outfit and white Forces, he looked to his left and openly sneered at the male guard beside him.

Labeled an out-of-control teen who would likely become a career offender, De'Marco's only aspiration was to follow in the footsteps of his older brother for whom he'd taken the drug charge. So, apart from making a name for himself through random acts of violence and intimidation, he would often be heard boasting on his brother's latest accomplishments in the streets - the sure signs of a recidivist.

"See you soon, Sanders." The guard smiled as the gate began to slowly retract.

"You'll see me in a casket before you see me back in a fucking cage," De'Marco declared in an earnest tone.

As he crossed the threshold of freedom, De'Marco tilted his head upwards and deeply inhaled, swearing it was true what people often said about the scent of the air being different.

"Young muthafucking Marco!" loudly greeted one of the two men who was standing before the shiny grille a Toyota Tundra.

Breaking into a broad grin, De'Marco gave a bear hug and handshake to the man he idolized: his big brother, Musa.

"Damn, li'l bro," Musa joked as they broke apart, "What the fuck was you up in there eating, *barbells*? Nigga, you feel like a slab of concrete."

The three men laughingly piled inside the Tundra, where Musa's driver took the wheel and De'Marco was offered the passenger seat.

Musa waited until they had reentered Detroit before leaning forward to toss a wad of money onto De'Marco's lap. "You held it down, li'l nigga. And this just a small token of my appreciation."

Wearing a large smile as he picked up the rubber-banded loaf, De'Marco was on the verge of voicing his gratitude when a gray crotch rocket appeared on the driver side of the truck. In black racing gear and a matching helmet, the rider removed a 30-round Glock from inside its leather jacket. Before either man inside the truck could react, the rider opened fire.

A hail of hollow points shattered the window, killing the driver instantly. As he slumped over the wheel, the truck swerved erratically before flipping several times and skidding to a stop on side of the road.

In spite of light traffic, the rider boldly braked beside the wreckage and hopped off. Jogging towards the Tundra, which was belly up, the rider fired four more rounds into the driver's corpse before marching around to the passenger side.

With blood gushing from various wounds, Musa and his brother had managed to crawl from the truck.

Musa shrieked in pain when the toe of the rider's boot broke several of his ribs. Due to the volume of treacherous acts committed in his past, he was clueless of the cause behind this brazen attack. But he was soon cured of his curiosity when the rider raised its visor.

His face instantly registering recognition, Musa shockingly stared into the merciless eyes of Kavoni McClain. Aside from orchestrating the robbery of Kavoni's drug house, Musa was the man responsible for sending him to prison for five years. So Kavoni found considerable pleasure in standing over him and his only sibling. Because now he had the privilege of killing two birds with one stone. Literally.

"Spare my little brother," Musa pled. "He ain't got shit to do with this."

Kavoni swung the Glock in De'Marco's direction and halted his heartbeat with multiple rounds, thus making the statement he made earlier appear almost prophetic. As Musa released an anguished wail, Kavoni silenced him with five rapid shots.

After a brief moment of glaring at Musa's disfigured face, Kavoni tossed the print-less pistol, then jogged back to the bike and climbed on. Revving the powerful engine, he dumped the clutch and caused the bike to take off in a wheelie.

While switching gears as he dangerously accelerated to nearly sixty miles per hour, Kavoni lowered the bike when it reached third gear and rocketed off.

***

Exhaust was softly exhaling from the tailpipes of a white Hellcat as it idled inside an abandoned warehouse. Calmly seated behind its tinted windows was Puma. Clad in dark clothing, one of her gloved hands was hugging the handle of a palm-sized pistol.

Puma received an incoming call, which she took through a set of Air Pods. After listening to the caller's brief instruction, she placed the pistol in her waistband and exited the car. Shortly after she raised a back door, the crotch rocket rolled inside and braked behind the Hellcat.

Dismounting the bike, Kavoni removed his helmet and quickly began stripping off the racing gear.

As he changed into a different outfit, Puma grabbed a gas can from the trunk and splashed its contents throughout the warehouse. Well-acquainted with wrongdoing, they knew the importance of eliminating all traces of physical evidence.

Before joining Puma inside the car, Kavoni retrieved a mini assault rifle from the trunk. Widely known as a Draco, he equipped it with a 100-round drum and racked an armor-piercing projectile into its chamber. With both feet firmly planted in the streets, his preference was to be judged by twelve, rather than carried by six.

The Hellcat was leaving the warehouse when its LED brake lights flashed. A second later, the passenger window lowered midway and Kavoni tossed out a sparked lighter.

Donning a pair of designer shades as the enclosure went up in flames, Puma turned onto a back road and awakened the Hemi.

Fumiya Payne

Chapter 15
Saturday night...

With Puma carrying a leather Goyard bag, she and Kavoni led their team towards the entrance of what was known as the livest strip club in the city. Draped in an impressive jewelry display and designer fabrics, all twelve felons were flaunting an exclusive pair of Detroit's signature eyewear: Cartier "Buffs".

Bypassing the mile-long line, Kavoni approached a club promoter and informed him of their reservation. As he was scanning the list, a woman nearby enviously eyed the entire team before her gaze settled on the solemn-faced patriarch. Along with him being handsomely clad in a Fendi button-down, fitted slacks, and Louis Vuitton loafers, Kavoni had the fresh cut of a man who recently rose from a barber chair.

Upon their admission into the club, where the atmosphere was pulsing with energy, all eyes were magnetically drawn in their direction.

"Bitch, that's them N.F.L. niggas!" one woman excitedly whispered to her friend as they marched past.

"Is it?" the friend asked in disbelief.

From their shameless savagery to the monstrous means of their overnight success, "The N.F.L." had been mentioned as maybe the deadliest crew in Detroit.

"Yeah, girl," the woman continued. "You see they all got them chains on."

The woman was speaking in reference to their massive medallions that were patterned after the N.F.L. logo. Encrusted with multicolored stones that twinkled like mini stars, it suspended from a Cuban choker the width of a pudgy finger.

As they settled within their reserved booths in VIP, King craned his neck to stare around the spacious establishment.

"Nigga, this bitch JUMPING!" he exclaimed.

Wearing a Balmain jacket over his sling-covered arm, Double-O nodded in agreement. "Yeah, it's definitely a lot going on up in here."

After being treated and released from a neighboring-city hospital for his gunshot wound, Double-O had declined the fixing of his front tooth. In his barbaric opinion, the war wound only complemented his creative craftsmanship.

On account of this being Kavoni's first public appearance since his release from captivity nearly a year ago, their booth was soon being visited by various villains who voiced their rejoice at seeing him. And because they're well aware of the excessive violence associated with his rise from famine to fortune, this was also an attempt at finding favor with the fearless figure.

Not one to overlook an opportunity, Kavoni capitalized on their cowardice by introducing them to Dolphin, with whom he encouraged them to shop.

The N.F.L. recaptured the spotlight as a fleet of bottle girls headed in their direction, hauling buckets of top-shelf champagne. At a value of well over five figures, a number of iPhones were being used to record the rarely-witnessed spectacle.

As his team was joyfully engaged in bottle-popping and lap dances, Kavoni's attention was seized by something across the room.

"I'll be right back," he said, excusing himself from the booth.

Puma motioned for Double-O to follow him.

Telling security a metal rod had been placed in his arm as a result of his gunshot wound, Double-O had been able to smuggle a small revolver in through his sling.

Inside the club's restroom, Kavoni stepped up to the sink as a tall, dark-skinned man was standing at the urinal.

"That nigga Freddie-D in there holding it down," Kavoni casually stated while washing his hands.

Caught off guard, the man at the urinal jerked his head in Kavoni's direction.

"He go up for parole next year," Kavoni continued, staring at himself in the mirror. "And the family only need fifty thousand for the lawyer. Which I think is reasonable, considering it's on behalf of a good man."

Flushing the urinal, the man turned to face Kavoni. "Brah, that ain't have nothing to do with me. So that's a conversation you need to have with my pops."

Kavoni smirked at his sarcasm. His "pops" had been dead over five years.

"You know, when I think about it…" Kavoni smiled, grasping the restroom door handle. "Maybe that's a conversation that should be had between father and son."

The man's father had once been a close friend to Freddie-D. until the pressure from a drug arrest was enough to expose the natural impurity of his heart. Sacrificing Freddie in exchange for a reduced sentence, he provided homicide detectives with detailed information on a cold case murder, a sin for which Kavoni and his former cellmate felt the son must make amends.

Whether it be in donation…or blood.

When Kavoni exited the restroom, he first spotted Double-O lingering nearby, then took in Puma as she stood by the bar with an attractive female.

This girl something else. He smiled to himself as they locked eyes.

Displaying her heavily-inked skin in a Givenchy V-neck, Puma had on a crisp pair of red Jordans and belted jeans that hung low on her hips. With a Pistons ballcap perfectly placed over four French braids, she definitely had more swag than the average male.

Kavoni signaled for them to join him back at the booth, where he questioned Double-O in regards to the caliber of weapon in his sling.

"It's a li'l .357, with the shaved hammer," he readily responded.

As Double-O could see the wheels of Kavoni's mind rapidly spinning, he leaned closer in eagerness. "What's on your mind, my baby?"

Removing his gaze from the booth in which the man from the restroom was seated, Kavoni turned to him and coldly stated, "Murder."

"It's now time for the main event!" the DJ announced, eliciting a loud reaction from the crowd. "And y'all in for a special surprise!"

The club was suddenly enveloped in a suspenseful darkness, with the exception of flashing strobe lights.

Then, as Future's song "Walk On Minks" began playing, the lighting was restored and two dancers came strutting down the catwalk in full-length minks, the matching hats, and oversized shades.

Upon reaching the stage, they began swaying to the music while teasingly undoing their coats. Before fully unveiling themselves, they dropped down and opened their legs to brandish bulges bigger than a baby's fist.

Bouncing back up, they shed the coats and posed before the crowd in Red Bottoms and lace thongs. Because they were both blessed with the voluptuous build of video vixens, it was difficult to decide on which woman to focus.

When they finally removed their hats and glasses, it was the dolled-up faces of Jazz and Unique.

Along with a dozen others, Puma and King were attentively planted along the edge of the stage; with both hands gripping bricks of money.

As part of a choreographed routine they'd spent hours rehearsing, Jazz and Unique stepped onto the mink coats and began to perform a provocative dance that would've impressed Cardi B. There was a continuous flurry of currency as they showcased their twerking skills both on and off the pole. Ending their performance on a high note, they positioned themselves on all fours. Then, while looking back at the crowd, they used their softly rounded cheeks to give the crowd a long round of applause.

Minutes after leaving the stage, they came back out to join Puma and King inside their booth.

"Did you enjoy the show, bae?" Unique smiled as she rested her soft bottom on King's lap.

"Girl, I just threw like twenty racks." He grinned. "So what you think?"

Placing her lips close to his ear, she purred, "I think I want to wake up in your arms."

Since the night of their initial encounter, King and Unique had been communicating on a daily basis. And although it'd been nearly two weeks, she had yet to drown him inside the heated pool between her chocolate thighs. With this being an uncommon obstacle for King, his frustration had been overridden by intrigue. But it now appeared as if his patience may have paid off.

Puma paused her conversation with Jazz and leaned over to nudge Kavoni, who was wearing a spaced-out look.

"What's up, my baby, you good?" she questioned.

Kavoni calmed her concern with a subtle nod, but he was actually in deep thought about the woman he'd met at Walmart. Mecca.

While he had managed to conquer life - at least in a street-level sense - there was a void in Kavoni that money alone was incapable of filling, which had led him to entertaining the idea of having a virtuous counterpart. One who came in the form of a desirable woman.

A woman like Mecca.

I gotta shake this shit, Kavoni scolded himself. And he had the perfect remedy.

When he glared in the direction of a dancer who'd been visually undressing him all night, she could feel the heat of his gaze and the two locked eyes.

Get your thick ass over here! he silently commanded.

As if he'd spoken through a bullhorn, she immediately stepped off the stage and sauntered toward him.

Glancing out the corner of her eye, Puma cracked a subtle grin as the dancer, Dreamer, engaged Kavoni in a sensuous lap dance.

"So what you into?" Kavoni questioned her, hoping she would provide the right answer. Because any mention of drugs would result in her immediate removal from his presence.

Her bronze-colored breasts brushed against his chest as she whispered near his ear, "Cash, Cash-App, Chime, Venmo…"

Relieved by her response, Kavoni readily replied, "And I got all the above."

"A'ight, we wanna thank everyone for coming out," the DJ said, lowering the music. "But unfortunately, it's time to go. And you ain't gotta go home, but you gotta get the hell up outta here!"

As people were noisily exiting the club, two gunshots suddenly rang out and caused an instant stampede.

Among those fearfully fleeing across the parking lot was the tall, dark-skinned man from the restroom. And behind him was Double-O.

Although his right hand was concealed within his coat pocket, Double-O genuinely appeared to be running for safety.

As another set of gunshots rang out, the dark-skinned man fell face forward onto the pavement. With blood pooling from a large opening at the front of his head, he was dead before he hit the ground.

Double-O unsuspectingly ran past him and hopped in the passenger seat of a steel-gray Camaro.

"Well done," Kavoni commented as he shifted the car in drive and screeched off.

Proudly displaying his chipped tooth, Double-O grinned, "Now he just as dead as his rat-ass daddy."

Shortly before closing time, Double-O had gone to the restroom and transferred the gun to his coat. Then, as everyone was leaving, he slid a hand inside his pocket and fired toward the ground. The frenzy that followed allowed him to continue shooting through his coat while running with the crowd.

And with so many people scattering at once, coupled with the absence of a muzzle flash, the shooter could've literally been *anyone*. So while his course of action may have been bold, tonight's incident would surely be written off as an unsolved murder.

Chapter 16

After fleeing the club with Unique, King had driven to the downtown area, where he wheeled into the parking lot of The DoubleTree.

"What the rent like on this every month?" Unique asked as he killed the engine.

"The rent?"

"Yeah. This where you been living at, ain't you?"

"Hell naw!" he laughed. "But you said you was tryna kick it, so I just thought I'd get us a suite for a couple days." He reached over to squeeze one of her thighs. "You know, one of them top floor joints. That way everybody can't hear you scream."

Unique smirked. "Let me ask you something, King."

"Anything."

"And be honest."

"I'd do nothing less."

Slightly turning in her seat, she asked, "Do you think of me as wifey material?"

"Absolutely," he truthfully answered. "Because not only is you gorgeous, but you the first girl I've actually spent time with and really gotten to know. So hell yeah, I can see you being wifey!"

"Well, let me put you up on game, li'l buddy," she said, patting his thigh. "You take *hoes* to hotels…but spouses to *houses*."

"That's the first time I've ever heard that one," King laughed. "But nah, it ain't even like that for real. It's just, Kavoni don't like nobody knowing where I lay my head at, you feel me? Brah got trust issues."

"Drop me off, King," Unique said, turning to stare straight ahead.

"*Drop you off?*" he repeated, thoroughly confused.

"Nigga, if you can't trust me enough to let me inside your crib, then what the fuck makes you think I should trust you enough to let you inside my *whole pussy*?" Unique scoffed in disgust. "Yeah, you most definitely got me confused with some bum bitch. So like I said, drop me the fuck off."

During their quiet ride to southwest, King was inwardly convincing himself that she was unworthy of the hassle. Nigga, it's a million hoes out here. *So fuck this bitch. Pussy pro'ly trash anyway.* But when he pulled into her complex, King became frightened by the finality of their friendship and attempted to regain her favor.

"Hold up, yo," he said, grabbing her arm as she reached for the door handle. "Just hear me out real quick."

"What is it?" she replied in an irritated tone.

"Look, I'ma be real with you. I ain't never been with a woman as mature as you before. I'm used to getting what I want, on account of what I got. But with you, it's different. So I just be needing you to excuse some of my mistakes. 'Cause it don't be intentional. It just be me not knowing."

Unique could sense that King was speaking from his heart. So while she might not yet know his entire back story, she did know when a man was moldable, which would go a long way with what she had in store. Releasing the door handle, she turned to question him with a direct stare, "What do you want, King?"

"What you mean?"

"I mean, besides all the street shit, what does Kingdom McClain actually want out of life?"

A question he'd never been asked by himself or anyone else, King was unable to readily respond. But to salvage the friendship, he thought he had to come up with something. "I mean——"

"Don't worry about the answer right now," Unique said as she laid a consoling hand on his forearm. "Because it's something you should be able to answer without hesitation. But, King, if you gon' deal with me, then I'ma need you to start taking life more serious. Because I got plans bigger than dancing and dating dope-boys."

His receptive expression was enough to make her inwardly smile.

"Come on," she said, opening her car door. "Let's go in the house."

Once inside her small apartment, which was nicely furnished, she instructed King to make himself comfortable while she took a shower.

King was scanning through the TV channels when he tossed the remote aside and went upstairs. With steam seeping out into the hallway, he opened the bathroom door and stepped inside.

Unique peeled back the shower curtain as he was removing his shirt.

"Boy, what you doing?" she giggled.

"Shid, I wanna get clean too," he answered, then stepped out of his boxers.

"Mmph," she grunted, impressed by a package she prayed could provide excessive pleasure.

Inside the shower, as they took turns bathing each other, King palmed her bowling-ball-shaped cheeks and aggressively drew her close.

While engaged in a sexually-starved kiss, Unique could feel his pulsing pole pleading for permission to penetrate.

"Please tell me you got some protection," she huskily breathed in his ear.

"I don't," he said, planting passionate kisses along the column of her neck. "You?"

"Nothing that's gon' fit."

"Girl, I swear I'm cleaner than the Board of Health," King certified.

"And I ain't saying you ain't," Unique moaned as his lips continued their sensual assault. "But bae, I can't risk it."

Respectful of her discipline, King nodded in acceptance.

But refusing to fully release her from his hooks, he knelt down and draped one of her legs over his shoulder.

As her clitoris began to throb in anticipation, Unique shakily inquired, "Boy, what you 'bout to do?"

Before lapping up her honey with kitten-like licks, he looked up and smiled. "Something I wouldn't do to a hoe."

***

MEANWHILE...

"Why is you fucking me like this!?" Dreamer screamingly demanded as Kavoni had her suspended in midair, mangling her insides in a merciless manner.

Besides his shoes and jewelry, Kavoni was nakedly planted in the center of a hotel room. Showing no signs of exhaustion as he gripped a handful of her loose cheeks, he was bouncing her up and down at a forcefully-rapid pace. With her arms tightly encircled around his neck, Dreamer was enjoying every pleasurable stroke of his painful performance.

"Let me suck it, daddy!" she suddenly pled. "Let me put that fat dick in my mouth!"

She ain't gotta tell me twice, Kavoni thought as he eagerly ejected his erection and lowered her to the floor.

Quickly kneeling before his pole, she snatched the condom off and surprisingly swallowed him whole.

"Ohhh SHIT!" Kavoni squealed in surprise. He'd had his fair share of women, but none who had been talented enough to bypass the warmup stage.

With the head lodged in her throat, she made several gulping sounds before slowly dragging her luscious lips to its tip, leaving a thick trail of saliva along the long road of his shaft.

"I love sucking dick," she breathlessly confessed, then lovingly circled her pierced tongue around the head and savored the sweetness of his pre-cum. "He so thick and beautiful," she praised, aggressively slapping it all over her face.

While staring up into his eyes, Dreamer fully extended her tongue and forced him back down her throat. Fighting off the urge to vomit as her flared nostrils were nuzzling his pubic hairs, she opened her mouth wider and made room for his balls.

In disbelief of her extraordinary feat, Kavoni had no choice but to reward her with a stomach full of protein.

After she literally sucked him drier than the Sahara desert, Dreamer looked up at him and tearfully smiled. "I could drink that for breakfast, lunch, and dinner."

With the stamina of a professional soccer player, Kavoni chewed open another condom, which Dreamer used her mouth to apply.

"Bend this fat ass over!" Kavoni barked, roughly smacking it.

When she obediently complied, the steep slope of her spine reminded him of the women's magazines he had masturbated to when in prison.

As he aligned himself with the opening of her meaty lips, Dreamer looked over and shoulder and moaned, "Please, don't hurt me, daddy."

Knowing fully well this was her way of telling him to do nothing less, Kavoni dug his claws into the satiny skin of her cheeks and delivered the discipline she so desperately desired.

Fumiya Payne

Chapter 17

With Jazz behind the wheel of a Trackhawk, she and Puma pulled into the driveway of Kavoni's condo.

He and his four-legged fighter exited the house moments later and joined them inside the Jeep.

"Change of plans," Kavoni announced as he reached for his seatbelt. "We gotta shoot to Kentucky instead."

While the dogfighting event was initially scheduled to take place in Indiana, Kavoni recently received a text that informed him of a last-minute location change, which was not uncommon in such a loathed and illegal sport.

As the Jeep was flying down 7-Mile Road, two Chargers emerged from a side street and fell in behind it. Scanning her side mirror, Puma knew Double-O and King were in one vehicle, and in the other were a pair of piranhas who'd plug the Pope for pennies.

Before jumping on the interstate, Kavoni had Jazz stop by a small house off 7-Mile and hit the horn.

An older man with a slim build and graying hair came out shortly after, carrying a plastic grocery bag.

"What's going on, youngster?" he greeted Kavoni upon climbing into the Jeep.

"I'm well, how about you?"

"Glad for the ride!" the man smiled. "So again, gratitude for bringing me along."

With decades of experience beneath his belt, the man, Ricky Malloyd, was once known as one of the best "dog handlers" in the state of Michigan. Having just completed a ten-year sentence for armed robbery, Kavoni had offered him a less dangerous way of earning a steady income.

"So what you thinking?" Malloyd asked as they sped down the highway.

Kavoni looked down at Squeeze, who looked up to meet his gaze.

"I think he'd rather die than disappoint me."

In addition to the rigorous training and high-protein diet, Kavoni had connected with Squeeze on an unusual level. So much of his calmness could be attributed to a phenomenal technique he'd soon expose.

When the convoy arrived in Covington, Kentucky, the GPS led them to a rural part of the city, where a number of cars were parked outside a barn-like structure.

Kavoni placed Squeeze on a leash and exited the 'Hawk.

As King and two others emerged from one of the Chargers, Kavoni couldn't believe his eyes. Along with Double-O, Unique was also present.

Handing Malloyd the leash, Kavoni approached King and draped an arm around his neck.

"Brah, let me rap with you real quick," he said, leading him out of earshot.

"I already know what you thinking, bro," King quickly stated. "But trust me, this bitch solid."

"Brah, you don't even know her!" Kavoni replied, struggling to keep his voice down.

"We didn't know Jazz, either," King shot back. "But now she know about bodies and everything. So what's the difference?"

Although he had a valid point, Kavoni would never admit that his real reason for mistrusting her was based on King's general weakness when it came to women. The boy had a gentle heart, which often allowed him to excuse inexcusable flaws. So until Kavoni's instincts said otherwise, there was no room for Unique at his table.

"I'm sorry, my baby," Kavoni said, shaking his head, "But I can't vouch for her."

"So what the fuck I'm supposed to do, leave her in the car?"

While that was definitely an option, Kavoni had a better idea.

"How much bread you got?"

"I don't know," King shrugged, "Pro'ly like a few hunnid. Why what's up?"

Kavoni reached in his pocket and pulled out a few thousand.

"Here," he offered it to King. "They got a mall downtown. Take her shopping."

King stared at the money for a minute before he surprisingly declined it.

"I'm good, bro." He shook his head. "Because that don't change the fact that you putting me in a fucked-up position. 'Cause now she gon' feel like she can't be trusted or something."

"That's why you should've asked before you brought her," Kavoni stated before turning to walk off.

Retrieving the leash from Malloyd, Kavoni instructed the pair of piranhas to stay with King. "And Double-O, you with me."

As Double-O glanced at King before following orders, his eyes bore a reflection of empathy. He knew his friend didn't mean any harm. But it was not his place to dispute Kavoni's decision.

A match had just ended as they entered the building. Inside an enclosed pit the size of a boxing ring, one man was happily collecting the purse, while another sadly scooped up his injured animal.

Kavoni was approached by a facilitator, who took his info before showing him to his opponent.

Accompanied by two other men, the Tennessee native was the owner of a vicious-looking dog named Hit Man. With a block-shaped head and three white socks, the red brindle was just one battle away from being crowned "Grand Champion".

"What up doe?" Kavoni greeted with a slight lift of his head.

"Shid, that scratch line, potna," Tennessee bluntly replied. "So let's count this paper and get these boys washed and weighed."

This nigga a clown, Kavoni thought to himself. *And they known for trying funny shit.*

After fifty-thousand was counted and given to the referee in charge of the match, they exchanged dogs for the purpose of bathing them. The bath was simply to ensure that the fur was absent of any substances that would discourage their dog from making contact.

Kavoni placed Hit Man inside a tub, then stepped aside for Malloyd. Instead of a bath, the dog handler had a different method for substance detection. After washing his hands with a bar of unscented soap, he removed a gallon of milk from the grocery bag and slowly poured it over the dog until his entire coat was saturated.

Allowing the milk to settle for several minutes, Malloyd then ran his hand down Hit Man's back and licked his palm. He turned to Kavoni seconds later and shook his head.

"Your boy clean," Tennessee confirmed as he walked up and handed Kavoni the leash to Squeeze. "And if you want to, we can skip the weight and get straight to that box."

Kavoni grabbed the leash with one hand and withdrew a weapon with the other.

"Your mouth is one thing," he said, touching the tip of his Taurus to Tennessee's scalp. "But to think I'm sweet enough to be *finessed*. Nigga, I'd choose death row over disrespect, *any day!*"

A method Malloyd had learned long ago, the usage of milk would surface whatever substance that had been applied to the dog's coat. So once he ran a hand over Hit Man and licked his palm, the numbing of his tongue was evidence that the dog had been tampered with. And that was a claim on which he'd stake his life.

"My boy a four-time champ!" Tennessee angrily asserted. "So I ain't got no reason to cheat!"

Puma was holding Martha in plain sight as she closely monitored his men's movements. And no longer wearing a sling, Double-O calmly stood with a hand hidden within the pocket of his windbreaker.

Taking notice of the deadly scene, a facilitator rushed over to intervene.

"What's the problem?" he questioned Kavoni in a composed tone.

"Ask this clown-ass nigga," he barked without breaking his stare.

As several more facilitators walk up, Tennessee got loud. "Man, y'all better to get this nigga, mane!"

To calm the nerves of everyone present, a facilitator asked Kavoni if he would lower his weapon.

Warning Tennessee that the slightest shift would get him shot down, Kavoni lowered the gun to his side.

When Kavoni was again questioned in regards to what the problem was, Malloyd spoke up. "His dog ain't right."

As Tennessee feigned ignorance of any wrongdoing, a facilitator took Hit Man to a back room for testing. He returned moments later and affirmed that the dog was indeed unclean.

The referee was waved over and told that Kavoni was the winner by way of default.

Ignoring the earnings, Kavoni realigned his semi with Tennessee's face.

"Come on, mane, just take the money!" he pled in panic when Kavoni clenched his jaw as if bracing to fire.

"My dog came for a fight," Kavoni stated, "And that's exactly what the fuck he gon' get."

Including Tennessee, the facilitators frowned at his statement. Clearly, he didn't expect to prevail over a dog who was basically incapable of being bitten.

But his true intentions were revealed when he instructed Tennessee to remove his clothes.

"Since your dog can't fight," Kavoni coldly explained, "You gon' take his place. Now strip down to your draws before I blow your shit off."

As he peered into the soulless eyes of a cold murderer, Tennessee cowered beneath his stare and began to fearfully comply. When applying the substance to his dog's coat that morning, he never imagined his deception would desert him in such a terrifying position.

Once in his boxers, Tennessee was led over to the pit, where he was ordered to climb inside and get down on all fours.

Placing Squeeze in the opposite corner, Kavoni whispered something in his ear that instantly converted his calmness into rage.

With Puma and Martha continuing to keep a close eye on Tennessee's two men, Double-O was acting as the referee and stood in the center of the pit.

While some were stunned by what they were about to witness, others were nosily engaged in the placements of bets, with the majority on Squeeze.

"All the dog gotta do," one gambler said to another, "is get a hold of that nigga neck, and it's a *wrap*."

Double-O had to force himself not to laugh as he looked down at Tennessee, who was wearing white briefs and a terrified expression.

He turned to Kavoni and pointed. "You ready?"

His eyes staring straight ahead, he offered a subtle nod.

Without addressing Tennessee, Double-O yelled, "Go!"

Kavoni snapped the leash and Squeeze surged forward.

As the canine closed in, Tennessee held out his forearm. His plan was to give the dog something to lock on, then use his free hand to strike with.

But when Squeeze unexpectedly dipped beneath his arm and angled his head upwards, Tennessee released a piercing scream as his throat was suddenly caught within the dog's powerful jaws.

Cries of excitement erupted from the crowd as Tennessee was on the ground, squirming beneath Squeeze in agony.

"HELLLP! HELLLP!" he repeatedly screamed.

When Squeeze opened his mouth to take a bigger bite, Kavoni slapped the outside of his thigh and commanded, "Squeeze, *here!*"

The dog immediately surrendered his hold and joined Kavoni at his left.

"I got money on this shit!" one of the gamblers shouted, "So let 'em finish!"

And they call me heartless, Kavoni chuckled to himself.

While this was nothing more than a memorable lesson, Kavoni used his earnings for reimbursements.

Having lost control of his bladder and bowels, Tennessee climbed to his feet and shamefully scurried from the pit. Grateful to still be alive, revenge was the furthest thing from his mind.

As Kavoni was leaving, he was approached by a man whose aura smelled of power and importance.

"Excuse the intrusion," he spoke in a Spanish accent, "but your display was so full of character." Leaning closer, he whispered, "The character of a monster."

The man removed a business card from his inner coat pocket and handed it to Kavoni. "Because we know nothing of each other, that makes for good business. And it'll never be for anything beneath six figures."

After giving Kavoni a firm handshake, he rejoined his crew and exited the building.

"Yo, what was that about?" Puma nosily inquired

Kavoni showed her the business card, "Another source of income."

Fumiya Payne

Chapter 18

Beneath a clear blue sky, the Coney Island on 7-Mile was jam packed. A popular hangout for both genders, this hot dog establishment was widely known for how easily and often it had become a crime scene, which explained the permanent bloodstains on its pavement.

With the music blaring inside King's "442" Cutlass, Double-O was right-handedly steering it down 7-Mile. And dangling from the sunroof were King's legs, as he sat on the roof of the speeding car. As Double-O slowed the Cutlass and wheeled it into the crowded Coney Island, the sun beautifully highlighted the various colors of its chameleon-painted skin.

From his elevated position - courtesy of the car's 30-inch feet - King was rapping along with Tee Grizzley's song, "Left Wrist Icy".

"...ASKED GOD TO HELP ME TAKE FLIGHT/ NOW I KNOW HOW IT FEEL TO DO EVERYTHING EXCEPT WEAR FAKE ICE/ ONLY TELL THE TRUTH TO JESUS WHEN WE TALK ON LATE NIGHTS/ LIKE, YOU KNOW I COMMITTED EVERY SIN EXCEPT FOR RAPE, RIGHT?"

Basking in the crowd's attention as the Cutlass crawled through the lot at a turtle's pace, King was boldly brandishing a blue-steel Beretta like he was a licensed-to-carry citizen.

Double-O parked beside a Chrysler 300, where two women were seated within its leather cabin. Wedging twin Glocks in his waistband, he exited the car and locked eyes with the driver. When her gaze gravitated toward his neck, Double-O proudly smiled at the fear and fascination his N.F.L. chain elicited.

Climbing out the sunroof, King hopped down from the car and was coming to join Double-O when he saw something that stopped him dead in his tracks. Clad in gray leggings and a midriff top that exposed her pierced navel, Unique was grinningly engaged in conversation with some light-skinned pretty-boy. Enraged for a number of reasons, King marched in her direction.

Unique instinctively looked to her left and spotted King angrily coming towards her. With no time or choice but to confront the situation head-on, she prayed to herself, *Please don't let this nigga embarrass me out here.*

"What's up, 'Nique?" King questioned with an obvious attitude.

"What's up, King?" she coolly replied.

He eyed her for a minute, then turned to her company. "Aye bro, let me holla at this bitch real quick."

"King, you better watch your——"

"Shut the fuck up!" he barked before she could finish her statement.

"Come on, brah," her company cut in, "You can't be talking to her like that."

"Or *what*?" King challenged as he took a step closer. "Nigga, my name King. I'm a *original* member of the N.F.L. And I'll smoke yo' bitch-ass out here in front of *everybody*!"

"Will you please get him?" Unique pleaded with Double-O as he rushed over.

Because he sided with King whether he was right or wrong, Double-O decided to see in what direction the situation would head. And he'd scold his friend in the county jail if that's where it led.

Empowered by the presence of his partner, King removed the Beretta from the small of his back. "They say a good run beats a bad standing," he told the pretty boy, cocking back the hammer. "So what the fuck you gon' do?"

He held King's stare a second too long and the butt of the Beretta was brutally brought down on the crown of his head.

"Oh my God!" Unique covered her mouth in shock as he unconsciously crumpled to the concrete.

King grabbed her arm. "Let's go!"

Allowing herself to be pulled along, Unique was secretly stimulated by King's savagery.

The crowd parted like the Red Sea as they came through.

As Double-O reclaimed the wheel, King protectively placed Unique in the backseat before hopping up front.

Whipping the wheel to his left as reversed out into the street, Double-O threw it in drive, then smashed the gas and painted the pavement with a pair of purplish prints from the Pirelli's. With its back-end slightly fishtailing, the tires gained traction and the screaming Cutlass flew off down the block.

After stopping for Chinese takeout, Double-O delivered King to the doorstep of a fenced-in house off 6-Mile and Gunston.

"A'ight, my baby," King said as he and Double-O dapped up, "I'll see you in the A.M."

Double-O responded with only a subtle nod, unsure if King was making a crucial mistake by disclosing the location of his home to Unique. As he thoughtfully watched King and Unique disappear inside the house, Double-O's attention was diverted by an incoming text message.

OMW, he readily texted back, then cast another glance at the house before speeding off.

Because King's house bore a deceptively-moderate exterior, Unique was pleasantly surprised by the stark contrast of its interior design. From the leather furniture to the high-end appliances, she knew a pretty penny had been invested into the plush-carpeted home.

"Bae, who put all this together?" she inquired while admiring the colorful fish inside a large tank.

"Kavoni hired some lady from Ohio," he answered, bending over to remove his shoes.

Of course he did. Unique smirked to herself.

"Come on, let me show you something." He grinned mischievously.

Unique was blown away by the master bedroom. Aside from the theatre-size TV that was mounted on the wall, there was a massive bed in which at least six people could comfortable sleep. Her eyes were suddenly drawn to his dresser, where the screen of an Apple desktop showed sectional images of the house's outside perimeter.

"Let me guess," she said. "This was your brother's idea, too."

"Hey." He smiled, raising both hands. "I told you bro got trust issues."

Despite King being an adult, Kavoni's wish was that they remained under the same roof. But after persistently voicing his desire for privacy, King eventually convinced him to assist in the purchasing of his own property. The security cameras had been part of their compromise.

"I'm saying, though." King pulled Unique into his arms, "You still ain't told me why you been ducking my calls and shit."

Prying herself from his embrace, Unique stepped back to eye him with a disbelieving expression. "You really don't get it, do you?"

"Get what?"

"The fact that I need a *man* in my life, King. Not some little boy who follows his big brother around and goes with whatever decisions are made for him."

"So that's really how you see me?" he asked in an offended tone.

"What other choice do I have, when that's the picture you presenting? It's like you can't make a move without that nigga's approval. Do you know how embarrassing that shit in Kentucky was?"

After being denied access into the dogfighting event, Unique was heated. Demanding the immediate return to her apartment, she grew even more furious when King refused her request on account of not wanting to further upset Kavoni. It was in that moment she decided to discontinue all contact with him upon their arrival back in Detroit.

"Listen to me, King," Unique said, placing a hand on his cheek, "You definitely cool peoples. But, boo, you ain't ready for a woman like me."

He knocked her hand away. "So you think I'm just some lame-ass nigga, huh?"

"Not at all." She shook her head. "I just think you failing to live up to your *name*. So at some point, you gotta decide whether you gon' step up, or stay content with living in your brother's shadow. But me being the queen I am, I'm sorry, bae, I can't settle for the servant."

Wearing a thoughtful scowl as he slowly took a seat, the impact of her words assembled with feelings that were already written on the walls of his heart. For so long, he'd longed to make his own mark. He'd just never known where to begin.

As she could sense the internal war in which he was engaged, Unique walked over and cupped his chin in her hand. "King, look at me," she said, lifting his head.

When his teary eyes reluctantly rolled upwards, she softly encouraged, "Tell me what you're thinking, baby."

"You wouldn't understand," he said, slowly shaking his head.

Unique sat down beside him and took his hand. "I really care about you, King. And not on the elementary level you're probably used to, but on the level where I want to push you to go far in life. Because you a good man, and you deserve to live according to your character. But you gotta learn to trust me, bae. I know you've ever heard the saying, 'behind every strong man is an even stronger woman'."

He nodded.

"Well, baby, that woman right here, sitting beside you. And I'm not trying to replace your brother. I just don't want to see you miss out on your blessing. Because you never know when life will deal you another one."

Swayed by the sentiment of her speech, King buried his face in her bosom.

"Tell me what's wrong, baby," she crooned, gently rubbing a hand over his dreads.

"I ain't never had a mama," he confessed into her cleavage, "And my daddy hated me. So Kavoni was like both parents to me. He raised me."

As tears slowly slid along his cheeks, he looked up at Unique and confided, "And if it wasn't for Kavoni protecting me, I probably wouldn't even be alive right now."

Fumiya Payne

Chapter 19
FLASHBACK...

With his head down and hands prayerfully clasped, an older man was nervously seated in the waiting room of a city hospital. Beside him was his five-year-old son, who was observing his father through inquisitive eyes. Startling the child, the man leapt to his feet as a doctor entered the room.

"Doc, please tell me everything went okay," the man pleaded with a desperate expression.

"I wish I could, Mr. McClain," the doctor replied. "But unfortunately I have to inform you that your wife didn't make it."

As his posture visibly slumped in defeat, David McClain began to quietly weep. How could he possibly go on without his beloved Sherice?

"However," the doctor continued, "I do have some g——"

Before he could finish his statement, Mr. McClain abruptly walked off.

Unsure of what to assume as he watched the bereaved husband disappear around a corner, the doctor turned to face the little boy.

"Do you understand what's going on?"

He slowly nodded. "My mama went to heaven."

"Yes." The doctor offered a sad smile, "She definitely did." The doctor suddenly had an idea. "What's your name, young man?"

"Kavoni."

"Well, Kavoni..." The doctor extended his hand. "Come on. I want to show you something." Upon reaching the hospital's maternity ward, the doctor led Kavoni into a nursery full of newborns. Approaching a small crib, he lifted Kavoni in his arms and pointed down at a sleeping baby. "Kavoni, I want you to meet your baby brother, Kingdom."

Fully aware of the complications she'd encounter during the birth of her second child, Sherice McClain had made certain arrangements in advance. One of them was naming her unborn son in accord to her spirituality. Her hope was that it would provide some sort of godly protection over him were she to pass away. And little did she know, he'd most definitely need it.

As the doctor lowered Kavoni to the floor, he squatted down so that they were eye level. "Your mother wanted me to tell you something just in case she had to go to heaven. You want to know what it is?"

Kavoni quickly nodded.

"She said to tell you that if anything happened to her, she would expect you to make her happy by always looking after your little brother. And that she'll be watching you from heaven to make sure you're doing your job."

Kavoni considered his statement before turning back to the small crib. And when he got up on his tiptoes to peer inside, to his surprise, Kingdom's big brown eyes were watching him.

As the two siblings shared their first moment of bonding, young Kavoni inwardly vowed to uphold his duty with every bone in his five-year-old body.

Once Kingdom was brought home from the hospital, it wasn't long before their father began to openly express his dislike for the child - a child he blamed for the death of his wife.

"You better get in there and shut that nigga up," he warned Kavoni one night as Kingdom was wailing at the top of his lungs. "Because if I gotta go in there, he might not ever make another sound."

If it wasn't for the fear of being unforgiven when he reunited with his wife in heaven, Mr. McClain would've been dropped the baby off at the nearest orphanage.

Practically a baby himself, Kavoni ran into his room and tended to his brother. "You gotta be quiet, Kingdom," he said, gently picking him up. "Or that mean daddy gon' come in here. And I don't think he like you."

As if understanding the severity of their situation, his sobbing gradually subsided.

To avoid excessive contact with the baby, their father had taught Kavoni how to tend to his basic needs. So after changing Kingdom's wet diaper, Kavoni went into the kitchen to fetch an already-made bottle. While nestled in Kavoni's arms and greedily sucking on the nipple of his bottle, Kingdom's eyes never strayed from those of his big brother's. Once the baby had been fed and was then peacefully asleep, Kavoni crawled into his small bed, which was protectively placed directly besides his brother's crib.

As time progressed, so did their father's hatred. He'd now spank Kingdom with a heavy hand for even the smallest infraction.

One evening Kavoni was taking a bath when he heard his father threatening to kick the bedroom door open if Kingdom didn't unlock it.

Without bothering to dry off, Kavoni wrapped himself in a towel and rushed out the bathroom. "What's going on?" he questioned in concern.

"Boy, you better mind your damn business," his father growled. "Before you end up getting your ass whipped right along with his."

"I'm just asking what he did," Kavoni stubbornly persisted.

"Look!" Their father pointed toward the living room.

Kavoni turned to stare at the broken vase that had held their mother's remains - which were now scattered all over the floor.

"That's what the fuck he did!" he shouted.

Turning back to the bedroom door, he gave Kingdom one last warning to open the door. "'Cause boy, if I gotta knock this bitch down, I'ma beat you to death."

"I did it," Kavoni lyingly confessed.

His father regarded him with a wary eye. "You did it?"

"Yeah, I was chasing Kingdom through the house when I accidentally bumped into it and knocked it down."

Shaking his head, Mr. McClain responded, "I'm not buying that."

Kavoni shrugged. "I ain't got no reason to lie."

At 10-years-old, Kavoni now had the heart of a young lion. And he'd protect that cub on the other side of the door with his very own life.

"Boy, if you take the fall for this, I'ma beat you twice as bad as I was gon' do that no-good-ass nigga hiding behind this door."

Enraged by the last part of his statement, Kavoni used that rage to divert the attention from Kingdom.

"Nigga, I said I did it!" he shouted. "Ain't nobody gotta lie to your drunk ass!"

The beating that followed would appear nearly impossible to withstand.

Savagely striking an extension cord across his wet body, Mr. McClain treated his son like he would a stranger. And his exhaustion was the only thing that finally brought it to an end.

"Now let's see if you volunteer for some shit again," he coldly stated before leaving the house.

Painfully crawling to his bedroom, Kavoni called out his brother's name.

When Kingdom opened the door, he stared down in horror at the welts over Kavoni's tortured body.

As he began to cry, Kavoni mustered the strength to protectively pull him into his arms.

"It's okay, Kingdom," he weakly consoled. "'Cause I promise I will never let him hurt you.

***

Deeply touched by his heart-wrenching history, Unique then understood the bond between King and his brother. But she also understood how desperately he wanted to experience a woman's love, which was something Kavoni simply couldn't provide.

"Baby, I'm so sorry you had to go through all that," she said, wiping away his tears. "But I'm here now, and I'll never leave your side."

Standing up from the bed, King used his shirtsleeve to dry his face.

"Look at me." He laughed in embarrassment. "Up in here crying like a baby. You pro'ly really think I'm corny now."

"Nah, bae, you far from corny. I witnessed that earlier."

That earned her a slight smile.

"But for real though, King," Unique said, pulling him back onto the bed. "It's about to be us against the whole world, bae. And I'ma give you everything you've been missing in your life. But there's certain things I can't accept. And that's cheating, or allowing *anyone* to interfere with our relationship." As an expression of unease appeared on his face, she asked, "What is it, bae?"

Staring off into space, he dreadfully answered, "Kavoni ain't gon' be feeling this shit. And I don't know how else I can eat."

Unique moved to get up and he quickly grabbed her. "Where you going, girl?"

"Nowhere," she smiled, then sank to her knees.

King's heartbeat instantly quickened as she began to tug at his belt buckle.

Oh. My. God! he exclaimed to himself in excitement.

"Stand up," she ordered once his jeans were unfastened and around his ankles.

Eagerly obeying, he stepped out of the pants legs and stood before her in Under Armour briefs. King nearly fumbled at the goal line when she leaned forward and gently bit his bulge through the cotton material. He jumped back as if struck by a jolt of electricity. "Hold on, girl, you gon' fuck around and make a nigga nut too soon, and I wanna enjoy this shit."

"Baby, I got plenty of this in store for you. So let that be the least of your worries."

With that said, she removed his briefs and proceeded to feast on his curved piece like it was the Last Supper.

As King's lips were blissfully parted and his head atilt, Unique suddenly released him from her mouth with a loud plop.

"I'm down here, not up there."

When he woozily looked down, she commanded, "Now watch your bitch work."

The eye contact, coupled with the loud slurping noises, quickly became unbearable, and King warned her of his oncoming load.

She became the owner of his heart when she stuffed him down her throat and greedily gulped every spurt of his protein-laced sperm.

Slowly freeing him from her oral imprisonment, Unique gazed up into his lustful eyes and stated, "I got a way for my King to eat…if you down."

Chapter 20

Inside the basement of a gambling house on the west side, a hooded Puma was knelt down as she held a loaf of money in one hand and a pair of dice in the other.

"Bet another thousand I straight six." She looked up at her opponent, while rattling the dice inside her small fist. When it came to shooting craps, this girl was just as passionate and experienced as Kavoni was with dogfighting.

"Bet," he called, dropping a variety of bills onto the carpeted floor.

Puma looked over her shoulder at Double-O, who was watching over her with a solemn expression.

"How many bodies you got now, my baby?" she questioned.

"Six," he truthfully admitted.

"Yeah, that's what I thought," she smirked before turning back around.

Releasing the dice with a fancy flick of her wrist, Puma snapped her fingers and yelled, "Double-O!"

When the tumbling cubes tired out on five-and-one, the volume of the crowd's reaction was deafening.

Since texting Double-O for his assistance, this was where Puma has been patiently planted. Because if there was one thing she knew about this game, it was that the richest person present usually prevailed in the end. And with her money being as long as train smoke, she was confident it was only a matter of time before she broke the bank.

As Puma was reaching out for the dice, her sweater rose up in the back and exposed the handle of Martha. Several people slightly stepped back at the sight of the full-size Glock.

Puma was shaking the dice, when she felt the vibration of her ringing phone. Reaching inside her hoodie, she removed it to see that it was a call from Kavoni.

"What's good, my baby?" she immediately answered.

After listening to his brief message, she replaced the phone in her pocket and began scooping up her winnings.

"Aye, y'all, I gotta go," she announced in a hurried tone, evoking a slew of murmuring obscenities.

"Hellll naw!" one man cried in objection. "How the fuck you just gon' take all my money and dip?"

"Dip?" Puma frowned. "Nigga, I've been down in this basement for damn near three hours. Fuck you want me to do, stay down here all night?"

"I'm just saying..." he shrugged. "At least give me a chance to get my shit back."

Puma sighed in irritation.

"How much money you got right there?" she asked, nodding at his hand.

He slowly counted it before mumbling, "Eight hunnid."

She dropped eight bills on the floor. "Bet that whole eight I strike on the first roll."

The man's eyelids began fluttering in nervousness, for his last eight hundred dollars was the rent money. And his baby mother would act a complete fool if he returned home empty handed.

As the crowd was egging him on, two men quietly exited the basement.

Growing impatient, Puma sweetened the deal by dropping eight additional bills onto the floor. "Either you gon' doo-doo, or get the fuck off the pot."

Chances make champions, the man foolishly told himself before wagering his rent money.

"They got a homeless shelter around the corner," Puma joked while shaking the dice. "And they'll let you in if you get there before midnight."

Amid scattered laughter, she released the dice, yelling, "Crumbs and bums!"

"Ohhhh!" the basement erupted when she rolled an eleven.

Stuffing the money inside her backpack, Puma looked up into the man's disheartened face and shrugged. "You should've let me leave."

As she and Double-O were climbing the basement steps, they withdrew their weapons before stepping out into the darkened streets. Regardless of their body count, they were fully aware of the dangers associated with a vulture's appetite. They were marching towards her rental when Puma suddenly stopped and placed a warning hand in front of Double-O. Signaling for him to be quiet, they raised their Glocks at the Trackhawk, then glanced over their shoulders while beginning to backpedal.

While she had no idea of who or how many it was, Puma was certain that larceny was lurking on the passenger side of the Jeep.

Disappearing between the recess of two houses, she and Double-O ducked off inside a twenty-four-hour laundry mat, from where Kavoni soon picked them up.

"What happened?" he questioned no sooner than Puma closed her door.

"Bro, I can't even explain it." She slowly shook her head. "But my Spidey senses just started going crazy. I don't know if I was tweaking or what, but something just made me stop dead in my tracks."

Unbeknownst to them all, her instincts were indeed the only reason they were still breathing. Because crouched alongside the Jeep had been the two stickup men, who were bent on leaving them brainless for her backpack.

After dropping Double-O off at the Cutlass, Kavoni headed for the interstate.

"Girl, I can't believe you!" he openly scolded her now that they were alone.

"What?" Puma grinned, feigning ignorance.

"I'm not playing, Puma. 'Cause sometimes you be pissing me off with your arrogance. Like shit can't happen to you, or something."

Although she was secretly pleased by his brotherly concern, Puma sassily replied, "Bro, last time I checked, I was grown as fuck."

He briefly removed his eyes from the road to pin her with a piercing stare. "Don't let this shit happen again, Puma."

"Bro, I ain't never had no daddy, and it's damn sure too late to have one now."

Kavoni checked his rearview mirror before suddenly making a sharp U-turn in the middle of traffic.

Puma wore a confused expression as he pulled back into the laundry mat from which he picked her up.

"Get out," he ordered.

"Get out?" she repeated.

"Yeah, get your tough ass out my shit."

Puma scrunched up her face. "Bro, are you serious right now?"

"I'm saying, since you wanna be like the Lone Ranger out in this bitch, then you shouldn't have a problem figuring it out."

The two were wordlessly holding one another's stare when Puma looked away and scoffed. They'd had their fair share of arguments, but never to the point where he'd purposely place her within harm's way.

Puma turned to peer deeply into Kavoni's eyes. "So this really how you feel, huh?"

Kavoni averted his gaze and slowly nodded.

With the car's interior illuminated by the bluish glow from the dashboard, Puma was in absolute shock when she saw a single tear slowly slide down Kavoni's cheek. During their entire friendship, she had never witnessed this man exhibit *any* signs of weakness or vulnerability.

But then her shock was replaced by guilt, for Puma knew that her endangering behavior was the cause of his emotional grief. The thought of something happening to her was enough to bring this hardened killer to tears.

While they'd bonded on a number of levels, it was in this moment when she truly recognized the extent of Kavoni's love for her. And the sentiment of it seized her very soul. This, she knew, was the true feeling of unconditional love.

"Bro, I'm sorry," she said, laying an affectionate hand on his forearm. "And if I knew it would've worried you like this, I wouldn't have did it. 'Cause you all I got, my baby. So please forgive me, and I promise it will never happen again. You hear me?"

With the sincerity of her tone signifying her remorseful attitude, Kavoni had no choice but to nod his head in acceptance of her apology. This girl was like the little sister he'd do anything to protect.

As they were quietly riding down the interstate, Kavoni broke the silence with a nagging question.

"I mean, what possessed you to go to a dice game all the way on the west side, with just you and Double-O?"

"I can see how you'd be concerned, bro," Puma grinned, "But it wasn't just me and him."

Kavoni frowned. "It wasn't just you and him?"

"Nah." She removed the Glock from beneath her hoodie and held it up. "I had my girl, Martha, with me."

Kavoni could only smirk in amusement. Then he suddenly recalled another question he'd been meaning to ask.

"What made you come up with name Martha?"

Puma laughed, "After Martha Stewart, silly."

"Martha Stewart?"

"Yeah, Martha Stewart. Because what is she famously known for?"

Kavoni had to think for only a split second before he answered with a smile. "Cooking shit."

Fumiya Payne

Chapter 21
Chicago, Illinois

With her braided hair tucked beneath a ballcap, Puma was wearing blue work clothes as she sat behind the wheel of a mid-size U-Haul. The radio was playing at a low volume while she idled in the parking lot of a large shopping plaza.

After last night's incident between her and Kavoni, the two friends had stayed up into the wee hours of the morning, conversing directly from the depth of their hearts. Genuinely remorseful of her reckless behavior, Puma had taken the time to reiterate her sorrow and regret toward being his source of grief.

Sometimes a person can become so accustomed to something that they begin to unconsciously take it for granted. And just hopefully, it doesn't require a heart full of hurt to make them aware of their mistake. Which, luckily for Puma, it took only a small dosage.

For the passing of time, Puma selected random women she'd like to sexually convert if given the chance. *That's if they ain't already ready.* She laughed to herself.

Her game was interrupted by the ringing of a prepaid cellphone, which she readily answered.

"Domino's Pizza," she greeted.

After taking the customer's brief order, she brought the engine to life and eased out into traffic.

As she traveled down one of its main boulevards, she soon entered a gritty part of the large city. Turning down a side street that was lined with dilapidated houses and vacant fields, Puma purposely parked on the last block.

Quickly hopping out, she walked to the back of the U-Haul and raised its door, where the only thing inside was a wooden board and folded clothing.

***

At a self-serve carwash called Squeeky Clean, the parking lot was littered with a variety of people and shiny vehicles. But the main attraction was a six-figure Porsche 911. Miami-Blue over white interior, the GT3 was owned by one of Chicago's most lucrative drug lords, who was presently planted in its passenger seat.

With the sole of one shoe on the pavement and the other inside the Porsche, Tone-Lee was visibly enjoying the lingering stares and flattering comments. Under the watchful eye of twin mercenaries, the pint-size man had not a care in the world.

"Papi, I'm ready to eat," purred a pecan-complected woman from the driver seat. Her hair and makeup flawless, she was the younger sister of Tone-Lee's drug connect.

"Shit, I got a Polish sausage and two boiled eggs for you right here," he joked, gripping his crotch.

"Ooh, Papi, you so nasty." She playfully pushed him.

Tone-Lee leaned over to offer her his tongue, which she greedily accepted. Nearly a decade his junior, her lively spirit and whorish ways were as addictive as the drug with which he flooded the entire west side.

"So where my pretty lady wanna go?" He smiled.

"I was thinking Chipotle," she said, wiping traces of saliva from around her mouth.

"Then Chipotle it is."

Tone-Lee turned to lock eyes with the occupants of a cream Denali and twirled his finger in a "let's roll" gesture. Before closing his door, he waved in farewell as if a departing President.

His lady friend sped out of the carwash and stopped at a red light.

As the Denali was on the verge of pulling in behind them, a dirt bike came racing down California Avenue. Ridden by a lone rider, it suddenly swerved into the opposite lane and headed straight toward the Porsche's front end. Then, in a stunt of pure strength and boldness, the helmeted rider jerked the bike upwards and rolled onto the hood of the low-sitting sports car.

Squeezing the brakes so that the bike's front wheel rested on the car's roof, the rider's left hand swiftly swung a 30-round semi from within its jacket and dumped over a dozen rounds through the front windshield.

Unharmed, the female driver screamed hysterically at the sight of Tone-Lee's bullet-riddled face.

Tossing the murder weapon aside, the rider rolled over the hood of the Porsche and landed the bike back on the ground.

Shocked by the speed and ruthlessness of what they had just witnessed, the occupants of the Denali could only stare in awe as the dirt bike zoomed off down the street.

The twin brothers turned to look at each other and shrugged, both sharing the same sinister thought: HE REIGNED LONG ENOUGH.

***

Puma was still standing behind the U-Haul when she heard the sound of an approaching dirt bike. Grinning in relief, she quickly reached for the wooden board and adjusted it so that it served as a makeshift ramp.

When the bike cut through a vacant field moments later, it rolled up into the U-Haul and Puma slid the board in with it.

Now wearing a uniform similar to Puma's, Kavoni hopped out.

"You good?" Puma smilingly inquired, desperately wanting for him to divulge every deadly detail.

"Listen to you," he teased, reaching up to lower the door. "With your li'l nosy ass. You know they say curiosity killed the cat."

"Clearly you didn't hear the last part."

"And what was that?"

Puma smiled. "Satisfaction brought him back!"

Kavoni burst out in laughter. "Girl, what the hell I'ma do with your crazy self?"

As the pair pulled off in the U-Haul, Puma was all ears while he verbally relived every moment of his latest kill.

Fumiya Payne

Chapter 22

*"...And my heart cold, but you heat it up/ get you to the crib; lick it,
beat it up/ real power couple, they can't compete wit' us/ can't no
one fuck this up, 'cause it's too deep wit' us..."*

Slowly snaking her hips in synch with Li'l Durk's love song,
Unique was settled on top of King as they communicated with only
the use of their eyes. The two had awakened with an appetite that
food couldn't fulfill, so this was their idea of breakfast in bed.

Oooh, this dick feels so good, Unique thought to herself, biting
on her bottom lip.

Bitch, you better not ever leave me, King possessively replied.

As if capable of hearing his inward command, she consentingly
leaned down and drew his lips into a passionate kiss.

After their tongues had taken turns pinning each other down in
a sensuous wrestling match, she lifted her hips and began kissing
her way down his slender frame. Without breaking eye contact, she
removed the condom and lovingly licked from the bottom of his
balls to the peak of his pole.

In a competitive mood, King had her spin around into a sixty-
nine position. Face-to-face with a hairless peach that was as pretty
as its possessor, he ate the delectable piece of fruit exactly as he'd
been taught.

As they were competing for first place in a race to bring the
other to orgasm, King suddenly slid his tongue between the valley
of her soft cheeks and tickled the opening of her anus.

The euphoric feeling forced her to free him from her mouth and
gasp. "What are you doing back there, boy?"

Wordlessly continuing his oral onslaught, King was declared
the victor when he replaced his tongue with his thumb and jammed
it in her butt.

Unique screamed as she flooded his mouth with a nectar sweet
enough to cause cavities.

After thirstily swallowing every drop, King maneuvered from beneath her trembling body and mounted her from behind. While nibbling on the nape of her neck, he fed her every inch and began grinding at a forcefully-slow pace.

With a fistful of bedcovers and a pained expression, Unique loudly cursed him for the infliction of his blissful torture. It wasn't until King was filling her womb with enough come to create triplets that she realized he wasn't wearing protection.

"Damn, bae, I couldn't help it." He grinned in her ear. "That shit was feeling too good!"

"Boy, I swear if you get me pregnant and try to play me, I'm killing your black ass."

King laughed.

"Nah, I'm dead serious." She looked over her shoulder. "'Cause you could've easily pulled out. And you know I don't believe in abortion."

"Girl, the only way I'm leaving you is if I'm in a cage or a coffin. Other than that…" He kissed her temple, "I'm on deck till I'm dead, you hear me?"

"Yeah, I hear you." She eyed him with a solemn expression. "But just remember, I warned your ass, nigga."

After taking a joint shower and getting dressed, they grabbed two duffel bags before heading outside to his Cutlass.

"Let me see them keys, li'l buddy." Unique extended her hand.

"Girl, you don't know how to drive." He laughed. "You'll be done tore my shit clean up."

She playfully pushed him. "Boy, if you don't give me them damn keys!"

As Unique cranked up the car's powerful motor, King observed her from the passenger side with a subtle smile and the way her small left hand was clutching the chrome wheel as she leaned forward in her seat.

"Where your Glocky at, nigga?" She glared at him while gripping the gearshift.

Shaking his head in amusement, King removed the Ruger from his waist and laid it on his lap.

116

"Now let's get to this money," she said before whipping the steel slab out of her complex like a NASCAR driver.

With their pleasures fulfilled, it was now time to handle business. And their first destination was a rental agency, where they'd borrow a car less noticeable.

***

"I'm walking in now, baby." Unique smiled at her FaceTime caller while entering a jewelry store. "But I wish you could've been here with me."

Wearing oversized shades and a red minidress, she had a designer bag hanging from the crook of her left arm. She approached a glass display counter, where standing behind it was a male employee whose pale skin was marred by an aggressive case of acne.

"Hi, how are you?" Unique cheerily greeted him.

"I-I-I'm fine, and you?" he nervously stuttered, struggling to not to gawk at her braless breasts.

Unique smiled at his considerateness. "I'm well, thank you."

She then placed the phone against her chest and leaned forward to reveal in a secretive tone, "My boyfriend cheated, and diamonds are the only means of forgiveness."

He grinningly nodded in agreement, beet-red from the close contact with her perfumed cleavage.

"Yes, honey, I'm here." She beamed at the screen of her phone. "I was just telling this handsome young man to bring out the best. Because we're sparing no expense."

As Unique scanned the display case, she smirked in amusement when the employee attempted to discreetly place his hands over the growing arousal behind his zipper.

"May I see that one?" She pointed at a particular ring.

Upon its removal and placement in her hand, Unique inspected the ring before showing it to her caller. "It's decent. But I don't think it's big enough to make up for what you did."

Handing it back, she pointed out a second ring that was slightly larger.

"Oooh, this one is real nice!" she exclaimed while studying the lustrous gleam of its diamond. "I think I've found my best friend."

But when she informed her boyfriend of its price tag, her joyfulness instantly converted into anger.

"What you mean it's too fucking expensive?" she shouted, drawing the attention of other customers and employees. "Nigga, your trifling ass cheated on me. So clearly you don't think some little small-ass ring gon' fix this shit!"

Unique angrily disconnected the call before dropping the ring onto the counter. "He got me fucked up if he thinks I'm settling for less."

"I'm sorry for wasting your time, sweetie," she said to her wide-eyed admirer. "But I refuse to be mishandled by *any* man."

Pivoting from the counter, Unique pranced out of the store in a provocative manner, knowing fully well the employee's eyes were glued to the jiggling of her pantiless cheeks.

Outside the jewelry store, Unique approached the passenger side of a "Supersnake" Mustang and hopped in. Turning to the person she'd been on the phone with, she smiled. "Nigga, you got the baddest bitch in the world!"

"Is that right?" King teasingly replied as he shifted the car into drive and sped out of the parking lot.

Unique reached inside her handbag. "According to this, it is."

She was holding up the diamond ring that was allegedly too expensive for King to purchase.

When entering the jewelry store, Unique was already in possession of a counterfeit ring, which was hidden between her phone and the palm of her hand. So, after finding one that bore a close enough resemblance to it, she used the argument with King as a diversion to make the switch. And her sex appeal had simply been additional assistance.

"You know dog gon' get fired," King said in regards to the employee. "And they pro'ly gon' make him pay for that shit."

Unique grabbed his free hand and traced it over the soft contours of her curvaceous figure.

"A glimpse of all this chocolate was definitely worth seventeen thousand," she boasted, speaking in reference to the price tag attached to the diamond ring.

Fumiya Payne

Chapter 23

En route to Flint, Michigan, the rally-striped Mustang was howling down the interstate at ninety miles per hour.

Inside the car, King and Unique were holding hands as they sang along with Jay-Z and Beyonce's "Part II (Love On The Run)."

Since his acceptance of her business proposal, King and Unique had been glued to each other like Siamese twins. And to him, her ride-or-die behavior only solidified her worthiness in carrying his last name. So regardless of anyone's opinion, he intended to stick by this woman until he no longer had a pulse.

Arriving in a city dubbed as one of the deadliest in the country, Unique guided him to a section that was fearfully patrolled by even law enforcement. As they turned down a side street off Dayton Avenue, she pointed toward a beige house and instructed him to park nearby it.

Before exiting the car, King reached beneath his seat and grabbed a loaded firearm.

"You know there's no need for that, right?"

"I don't know these niggas." He wedged it in his waistband. "And you already know how they feel about niggas from the 'D'."

"Yeah, but these my peoples. And the same way I wouldn't let them harm you, I won't let you them harm them, either."

"You fighting a losing battle, my baby," King said, reaching for his door handle.

Approaching the front porch, they were confronted by a small group of men whose eyes were indicative of their experience with violence.

"What's good, Ni-Ni?" greeted the youngest of the bunch. Built like Stanley "Tookie" Williams, he appeared to have just stepped off the prison yard in San Quentin.

"Hey, Pee-Wee!" Unique smiled as the two engaged in a friendly hug.

Pee-Wee? King chuckled to himself. *Let me find out this nigga big as a house and soft as a mouse!*

"Pee-Wee, this my boyfriend, King," she said in introduction. "And King, this my li'l cousin, Pee-Wee."

Pee-Wee extended him a callused paw. "This a good woman you got on your arm, King," he leeringly stated with a firm shake. "And it would break my heart to see her hurt."

While his underlying threat wasn't lost on King, he assured Pee-Wee with a direct stare, "I'd murder the whole state of Michigan for this one right here, my baby."

As they ascended the front steps of the porch, King glanced to his right just before passing through the screen door. Coldly returning his stare was one of the scariest-looking men he'd ever laid eyes on, and lying across the lap of his army fatigues was a Russian AK-47 assault rifle.

Pee-Wee led them through the darkened house and into a small kitchen, where he retriever two green army bags from a deep freezer.

"This everything y'all asked for," he said, handing them to King.

Unique reached toward the back of her head and removed the diamond ring from within her hair.

With its price tag still intact, Pee-Wee regarded the small, sparkling ornament with obvious approval. After the deal was sealed with firm handshakes, Pee-Wee escorted them back outside.

"Fuck with me," he advised King before their parting of ways. "I can get my hands on all types of shit."

"I got you, my baby." He solemnly nodded. Risking another peek at the man on the porch, the intensity of his stare forced King to quickly look away. *That nigga ain't right*, he concluded to himself in uneasiness.

"And Ni-Ni, don't be such a stranger around here," Pee-Wee scolded her before reaching out for another hug. "Stop through sometimes."

"I will, cuz," she promised, leaning up to kiss his cheek.

As King and Unique climbed in the car with two bags that carried a federal indictment, he double tapped the horn when speeding away from the curb.

Stepping out into the street, Pee-Wee stared after the car until it was no longer visible, his expression a reflection of black ice.

Salute my Savagery

***

Safely arriving back in Detroit, King and Unique headed to her apartment, where they scampered inside and concealed both bags in the ceiling of her bathroom.

Unique excitedly wrapped her arms around King and planted kisses all over his face.

"Bae, the world ain't ready for us!" she exclaimed. "We 'bout to run the bag up and put this city in our rearview."

Along with their plans to infiltrate a higher tax bracket, the couple concluded that Detroit was a pond in which they no longer wished to fish. Their capabilities called for bigger catches, something an impoverished city was unable to provide. So, after a year-long run in the outer left lane, they'd exit somewhere in Atlanta, where the doors of opportunity were often opened to those who simply knocked.

There was a sudden knock at the front door, and King withdrew his weapon before descending the stairs. Peering out the peephole, he took in the lone figure and replaced the Ruger back on his waistline.

"What's good, my baby?" he smilingly greeted upon opening the door.

"What's good, brodie?" Double-O said, stepping into the apartment.

As they settled across from one another in the living room, King rubbed his palms together in excitement and enlightened, "I got a way we can get rich in six months."

Double-O regarded him with a leery eye. "Six months?"

"Bro, if we ain't got a million by March, I'll cut my nuts off."

Double-O smirked in amusement.

"Nah, for real, my baby," King earnestly insisted. "I'll literally take a blade and cut these joints clean off."

While he'd never expect King to actually castrate himself, Double-O could sense the seriousness of his spiel and grew more interested.

"A'ight, I'm listening," he said.

King wordlessly rose from the recliner and raced upstairs.

Returning to the living room with both army bags, he placed them on the coffee table and began removing their contents

Double-O's eyes instantly enlarged in awe and surprise.

In addition to handguns and assault rifles, there was an innumerable amount of ammo, drums capable of containing a hundred rounds, and body armor worn by law enforcement.

"This shit real?" Double-O questioned in disbelief.

King laughed. "For seventeen-thousand, it better be."

"Nigga, this the shit you see in movies," Double-O said as he picked up an AR-15 known as the "Witch Doctor". Equipped with a collapsible stock and dual-colored beams, the 5.56 assault rifle fired projectiles powerful enough to perforate concrete. "Where the hell you come up on all this shit at?" he inquired while staring through the scope and picking off imaginary targets.

"Up in Flint," King admitted, genuinely pleased by his friend's fascination.

Lowering the weapon, Double-O squinted his eyes at King. "Kavoni know about this?"

King grinned mischievously as he shook his head. "Nope. And I didn't use a penny of his to cop none of it, either."

Once they were reseated, King continued, "Don't get me wrong, my baby. I'm appreciative of everything bro done did for me, but he stunting my growth, Double-O. And I can't keep playing the sideline. So, I'm saying, let's get out on that field and call our own plays. Just me and you, my baby."

"What you got in mind?"

Leaning forward in a conspiring manner, King quietly outlined a vicious scheme to seize a sizeable section of the city.

When finished, Double-O eyed him with a contemplative expression, for he could partially foresee the aftermath of such a bold move. This could get real messy.

"I'm saying, bro." He leaned forward to peer directly into King's pupils. "Have you seriously thought about this?"

"I have." King nodded. "And it's time I stood from the support of my own two feet. And if bro can't understand my perspective, then that just goes to show how he really sees me: as just some li'l nigga who can't stay afloat without him. But as you can see…" King extended his hand toward the table, "That ain't the case, my baby."

"I hear you. But just know that if we move forward with this, ain't no rewind button. And it's a strong possibility that friends gon' become foes."

"Double-O, I love you like we came out the same pussy. So as long as I got you by my side, I don't give a fuck about nothing. And don't you feel the same about me?"

His eyes suddenly took on a menacing darkness. "Nigga, I'd go against God for you. So don't ever question my love or loyalty."

Even when King had frozen up on the night he'd gotten shot, Double-O never uttered a word of what happened to anyone. He truly loved King as a biological brother, and would never say or do anything to discredit his character. He was the epitome of a true friend.

Wholeheartedly believing every word of Double-O's statement, King had an outbreak of goosebumps.

As the two comrades gripped each other in a fierce embrace, Double-O solemnly stated, "If on the field is where you wanna be…then let's lace the fuck up!"

Fumiya Payne

Chapter 24

Kavoni's eyes were obscured behind gold Cartiers as he steered the Camaro through downtown Detroit. With a Sig Sauer within arm's reach, he was subtly bobbing his head to the sounds of rap artist Li'l Baby.

"...never running off, so if I owe you, I got you, I'll pay that/ give this shit my all, so when I'm old I can chill and just lay back/ really from the bottom, so in the trenches is where I feel safe at..."

Turning into a Popeye's Chicken, Kavoni idled behind a snow-white Braubus in the drive-thru line. He smirked at the car's license plate that read, *bosbich.*

"Hi, may I take your order?" a young woman's voice came over the intercom as he pulled up to the menu board.

"Do y'all serve blue cheese?"

"No, sir, we do not."

"A'ight, well let me just get a bucket of chicken. Extra crispy."

"Will that be all, sir?"

"Yeah, that's it."

"Alright, your order comes up to seventeen-thirty-six. If you'll please pull up to the next window."

Damn, she pretty as shit, Kavoni inwardly thought as he handed the young employee a twenty.

Along with his food and change, she wished him a good day.

"Yeah, you too." He winked before pulling off.

While waiting to merge back into traffic, Kavoni reached inside the bag and lifted the bucket's lid. And instead of there being extra crispy pieces of chicken, the box was filled with bundles of money, which was the payment for his stunt in Chicago.

The assassination of Tone-Lee had been sanctioned by his own drug connect, who had personally forbidden him from dating his baby sister. And as a lesson to her, he requested that she be shaken up in the process.

While Kavoni had never foreseen his involvement with contract killing, he had to admit that it was the easiest hundred grand ever made - not to mention the secrecy between him and his employer.

And in the words of the Puerto Rican contact he'd met in Kentucky, "That makes for good business."

Steering with one hand and texting with the other, Kavoni excitedly questioned Puma in regards to her current location. He couldn't wait to see her reaction when he offered her a piece of chicken and she saw what was in the box - half of which was hers.

Seconds after sending the text, the grille of a flatbed suddenly slammed into the passenger side of Kavoni's car, deeply indenting its fiberglass frame. A Ford work van then sped alongside the Camaro and skidded to a stop. Two figures hopped out, wrapped up like Taliban terrorists.

Barely clinging to consciousness, a disoriented Kavoni was feeling around for his firearm when his door was snatched open and he was put to sleep by a blunt object.

Quickly removed from the vehicle, Kavoni was caried to the back of the van and thrown inside, where two others in disguise began subduing his hands and feet. As the van sped off, Kavoni's car was being loaded onto the flatbed by two figures in hooded sweatshirts and sunglasses. Once finished, they casually climbed back in the tow truck and followed in the van's direction; leaving behind only shards of broken glass.

Several stunned eyewitnesses would swear the entirety of the incident occurred in under two minutes.

***

"I'm sure he's okay, Puma," Jazz assured her in a calming tone as they laid in bed.

Worriedly checking her phone every few seconds, Puma didn't respond. Instead, she swung her feet out of bed and started to dress.

After receiving a text from Kavoni, to which she immediately replied, she had yet to hear back from him. And that was nearly thirty minutes ago.

"Baby, where you going?" Jazz raised up in bed.

"I'ma just ride around for a minute."

"Puma," Jazz called out in concern.

She looked over her shoulder while slipping into a pair of gray Jordans. "What's up?"

"I'm saying, what, you just gon' ride around the whole city of Detroit?"

"Either that..." She shrugged, "Or until I hear back from him. 'Cause something ain't right. So if I gotta burn the engine out in my shit, then that's just what the fuck it is."

"But, baby, I guarantee you he good. He——"

"Stop saying that!" Puma thundered with clenched fists. "'Cause if he was good, he'd be answering his fucking phone. I don't give a fuck if he fucking a bitch, or whatever. This nigga ain't never ignored my call. Period."

Grabbing Martha, whom she didn't bother to conceal, Puma grimly exited the bedroom. As she was backing down the driveway, Jazz came running out the front door, waving for her to stop.

Puma reluctantly tapped the brakes. "What's up?" she icily inquired as Jazz hopped in the passenger seat. Nothing said would deter her from sliding through traffic.

"You my other half, girl," Jazz proclaimed in an earnest tone, leaning over to tenderly kiss Puma's cheek. "Which means your worries are my worries. So we'll burn this engine out together."

Puma nodded, deeply appreciative of her ally's allegiance.

While reversing out into the street, Puma was suddenly struck by a realization that made her slam on the brakes and reach for her phone. "How could I be so stupid!?" she screamed, recalling how she and Kavoni shared locations. In the event of an emergency or some other unforeseen occurrence, that was an arrangement they had made shortly after his release from prison.

Pulling up the "FindMe" app on her iPhone, she went to "people" and "navigation", then sped in the direction shown on her GPS. Led to a familiar location, her anxiety level lessened as she turned onto Jo'an street.

I'm 'bout to cuss this nigga the fuck out. She smiled to herself while parking in front of the house that served as their makeshift drug lab.

Telling Jazz she'd be right back, Puma tucked the pistol in her pants and excitedly exited the car. But when she ascended the front porch, her inward alarm was reactivated at the sight of Kavoni's abandoned phone.

Puma withdrew her weapon before quietly unlocking the front door. Then, pushing it open with the toe of her Nike, she cautiously crept into the house. After discovering it was empty, she stood in the living room, wearing a puzzled expression.

"Somebody gotta know something," she mumbled while reaching for her pone.

When King didn't answer, she tried Double-O.

"What's good, my baby?" he greeted after several rings.

"You heard from Kavoni today?"

"Nah, why, wassup?" he inquired, detecting the concern in her tone of voice.

As Puma was explaining what had provoked her state of panic, she heard King's voice in the background.

"Yo, where y'all at?" she questioned. "'Cause I just tried to call that nigga, King, and he ain't even pick up."

There was hesitation on Double-O's end before he replied, "We tucked off right now, my baby. But if I hear something from bro, I'll make sure he hit your horn asap."

"Aye, Double-O!" Puma hurriedly yelled, but the call had already been disconnected.

Puma reentered her car and angrily flung her phone at the front windshield.

"Yo, I swear on the life of every baby ever born!" she vented to no one in particular. "If a single hair was harmed on my bro's head, I'm wiping down whoever I think was involved!"

With the pronouncement of a promise she'd undoubtedly make good on, Puma had Martha in her grips as she sped off down the block.

Chapter 25

With watchful eyes and swift strides, Double-O exited a Dick's sporting goods store. Despite his presence in a public setting, he understood the importance in the coat of caution being constantly worn.

Approaching a Lincoln Navigator, he climbed into its backseat and settled across from a gorgeous young woman named May-May. Her complexion the color of almonds, the short-haired woman was a close friend of Unique's.

"Did they have 'em?" King questioned from up front in the passenger seat. Beside him was Unique, who wore oversized Chanel shades and a purple team jacket.

Double-O nodded in answer, removing a pair of HD binoculars from inside a plastic bag.

Steering them across town, Unique parked down the street from a one-level building. While it appeared to simply be a dance club, it was also the location of a high-stakes poker game. And despite a number of attempts, the place had never been successfully robbed.

Two hours before the club's opening, exactly as May-May had foretold, a set of luxury sedans slid into its parking lot. Double-O lowered his window midway and brought the binoculars before his eyes.

Exiting the vehicles in casual clothing were a total of four people, who at first glance appeared to be unarmed. But the slight bulge beneath two of the men's suit coats suggested they were carrying holstered firearms.

"That's the owner in all gray," May-May quietly pointed out. "And the two in back are his personal security guards."

Double-O took a mental photograph of the owner's face, then continued to observe the methodical movements of the two armed men. His gut instinct warned him of their gluttony for violence, which explained the number of botched robberies. So, if he was to pull this off, he'd definitely need to bring along the element of surprise.

"I thought you said they carry shotguns," he questioned May-May as the group disappeared inside the building.

"They do. But they already got 'em stashed somewhere in the club. Then when it opens, one of 'em be posted up by the metal detector, and another one be downstairs. Trust me," she emphasized, "These niggas ain't fucking around. I've seen 'em blow a nigga whole leg off and wait for the ambulance."

One of several women handpicked for the job, May-May served as a waitress in the well-guarded room where the gambling took place. As a single mother who struggled to make ends meet, she couldn't help but sometimes eye the stacks of money in a coveting manner. And while she could easily take advantage of the advances made by some of the solicitous gamblers, self-respect restricted her from doing so.

However, when the proposal of the place being plundered was presented to her, along with Unique's assurance that these were thorough thieves, May-May eagerly endorsed her signature. Her only request was that she receive ten percent of the take.

With Unique steering them through the city, Double-O was listening to May-May depict the club's layout and other security measures when he inwardly beamed as the means of their entry was suddenly revealed to him. And the man to help make it happen was already a member of their mini platoon.

When they dropped May-May off at her apartment, Double-O explained to her the strength of energy, and how important it was that she maintained a normal act of conduct while at work.

"I've been around violence all my life, li'l buddy." She patted his thigh reassuringly. "So I'll be just as calm as I am right now."

She was partially out the truck when Double-O called out, "And one other thing."

When May-May turned to face him, he solemnly stated, "I advise you to get real low when I come through. 'Cause these bitches gon' burn."

***

Later that night, King and Double-O sat alone in the Navigator as they were parked outside of Double-O's house.

"So you really rocking with shorty, huh?" Double-O questioned.

"I got to, my baby," King answered. "'Cause she rocking with me. And she ain't just talking it; she walking it. You feel me? Between me and you, she the reason I was able to come up on all them guns and shit."

King went on to disclose the finesse Unique had put down for the diamond ring, and how the proceeds were used to purchase the stockpile of weapons, ammo, and armory. "She was willing to catch a case to see a nigga get ahead, so how can I not acknowledge that for what it is?"

"I ain't knocking you, bro," Double-O responded. "Not at all. And if you happy, I'm happy for you. But don't never let yourself be rocked to sleep, you hear me? So if ever there's a sign you need to see, you won't miss it."

"What, you ain't feeling her or something?" King inquired. He knew Double-O had his best interests at heart, and would seriously consider his advice and judgement.

"It don't matter how I feel, my baby. So unless I was to personally see or hear something questionable about her character, then I'ma support whatever you wanna do. I'm just telling you to stay alert, that's all." In their line of work, Double-O knew it was mandatory that they maintained a sharp mindset, especially if they wished to prevail in a game where the retirement age began as early as adolescence. So he was simply encouraging King to remain watchful of everyone within harm's reach.

"So what you think about May-May?" King smiled. "She thick as fuck, ain't she?"

"She cool." Double-O shrugged in nonchalance.

"Come on, bro, cut the games." King playfully pushed him, "That bitch badder than a mu'fucka. And you already know I put in a good word for you, so I don't know why you ain't taking advantage. I bet her li'l shit pro'ly fire."

When Double-O didn't respond, King continued, "But for real, my baby, you gotta stop being so closed off with the hoes and learn to lighten up a li'l bit. You *all action*, bro. And that *can't* be good for a nigga, you feel me."

Throughout their entire friendship, King couldn't recall Double-O ever having serious feelings for a female. Part of it he knew resulted from the ridicule he received from certain girls in school, and the other half stemmed from the failed relationship between him and his mother. But. as a true friend, King just wanted to see him enjoy something other than the dispensing of violence.

"I'm good, bro," Double-O assured him. "'Cause trust me, at the level I'm playing at, a nigga can't afford no distractions. So you do your thing, and let me do mine."

Double-O's belief was that love could soften a soldier's savagery and dull the blade of his reasoning. He'd witnessed the effects of men who'd been weakened by women. How some had killed behind emotional feelings; crossed comrades with whom they'd had day-one dealings; ignored signs of deceit simply because she was physically appealing; and worse, snitching to avoid visiting prison. So though he occasionally engaged in sexual affairs, his heart was off limits while enlisted in the trenches.

"I'm just saying," King said in persistence, "At least get to know old girl. 'Cause you might end up liking her for real."

"I hear you, bro. But you know the only attachment I want is the one that come with a gun."

"Bro, you off the chain." King laughed. "We gon' have to work on getting some sunlight over that heart of yours. 'Cause that mu'fucka colder than Minnesota."

Double-O grinned. "Bro, you ain't never even been to Minnesota."

"Yeah, but I heard that bitch *freezing*!"

Chapter 26

Parked near a deserted waterfront, Puma was wearing dark clothing and a thoughtful expression as she sat on the hood of her Hellcat. Within arm's reach was her phone and Martha, as she attempted to arrange the assortment of thoughts by which her mind was consumed.

It had been over twenty-four hours since Kavoni went MIA, and Puma had yet to reconnect with either King or Double-O. While she hated to include them as possible suspects in his disappearance, their behavior had aroused a considerable amount of suspicion. But as she had already stated, she would exert every ounce of her energy into delivering death to all those responsible - whether it be friend or foe.

A habit in which she rarely indulged, Puma removed a small bag of marijuana from her pants pocket. Unable to eat or sleep, she was hoping the potent strand would at least decrease the degree of her distressed mind's state because she could presently feel herself slowly but surely coming unraveled.

As she was sprinkling the purple-haired buds across a Backwoods, her phone began vibrating inside her hoodie. Spilling the majority of the weed while quickly reaching for it, she was greeted with an image that left her breathless.

Hogtied and gagged, it was a picture of Kavoni. And for verification of it being recently taken, a masked figure was holding a sheet of paper with the date and written in large letters…the color of crimson.

Before she could regain her composure, Puma received an incoming call from an unknown number, which she readily answered.

"I'm assuming you get the picture," a male's voice chuckled in sarcasm. "And I'm also assuming this bitch-ass nigga worth $100,000. So be ready in like thirty minutes. And if you ain't coming alone, then don't bother coming at all."

Without giving her a chance to challenge the limited amount of time, the kidnapper disconnected the call.

Tossing the blunt, Puma hurriedly hopped back in her car and burned rubber.

Along the way to hers and Kavoni's stash house, she entertained a host of possibilities pertaining to the outcome of this situation. And in spite of the likelihood that she would lose both her life and the money, her love for Kavoni vaccinated her with the valor to willingly embrace whatever awaited.

As she exited the interstate, Puma carefully scanned her mirrors for any suspicious headlights. At this stage, paranoia could prove to be priceless. Although certain she wasn't being followed as she turned onto a particular street, Puma still circled the block before pulling into the driveway of a peach-colored house.

Once inside, she flicked the light switch and froze at the sight of the ransacked house. Quickly placing her back against the wall, she listened for any sounds of movement.

After several silent seconds, she rushed over to the wooden staircase that led to the top floor. She paused on the fifth step and bent down to jerk the board of the sixth tread. Held intact by only the strength of a strong magnet, the board lifted up to reveal a secret compartment that contained stacks of money.

Puma and Kavoni had considered several places in which they could stash their savings before she suggested the staircase. She had sensibly explained how its openness would work to their advantage. "Niggas will run up and down these stairs all night before they think to look in 'em," she suggested with confidence. Because Kavoni could think of no reason to disagree, the staircase became the secretive site of their wooden safe.

Puma removed five stacks of money and closed the contraption. Then, after casting a cautious eye out the window, she attentively exited the house.

In exactly thirty minutes, as she was idling in the parking lot of a restaurant, her phone rung.

"Where are you?" the kidnapper questioned.

Upon giving her location, she was told to drive to a nearby Walmart and park in the center of the lot.

Her phone buzzed minutes after her arrival, and she was given instructions to take the money to the women's restroom and place it inside the trashcan.

With the kidnapper staying on the line as she complied, Puma then demanded to know the location of Kavoni's whereabouts. "I gave you the money. Now tell me where my peoples at."

His response sent chills down Puma's spine. "Check the green car beside you."

As the call was disconnected, Puma snatched up Martha and scanned her surroundings. But the packed parking lot meant the culprit could be in any number of vehicles.

Slyly shielding Martha along her leg as she exited the car, Puma walked around to the driver side of the green Cutlass and leaned to peer in at an empty interior. After glancing over her shoulder, she opened the door and quickly reached to pull the trunk release lever.

With her heart racing as she approached the back of the car, she unconsciously held her breath and raised the trunk. Her hopeful spirits instantly sank at the sight of the vacant enclosure. Then, as she was on the verge of turning away, something shiny caught her eye. Lying off in a corner was Kavoni's gold-framed Cartier glasses, the same pair she purchased for his last birthday.

Angrily slamming the trunk, Puma ran back into Walmart. Not only was the money gone, but not a soul was present inside the restroom.

"Fuck!" Puma screamed, knocking over the trashcan. While this was one of the possibilities she had entertained, she'd been hoping that an encounter with karma could be postponed. But from the signs being shown, their paths were on the verge of crossing, and she was powerless in preventing it.

Uncertain of her next move as she aimlessly rode through traffic, Puma periodically peered at her phone, praying it would ring. Because should the kidnapper request a second ransom, she'd pay it without hesitation. Even if it only remotely meant saving Kavoni's life, she'd fork over every cent of their savings.

Puma made a sudden U-turn in traffic and sped off in the opposite direction. Arriving at Kavoni's condo, she used her key to gain entry and deactivated the alarm, which was a combination of their birth dates.

"Squeeze!" she yelled out in the eerily silent house. She'd been so distraught by this experience that she'd forgotten about the dog.

At the sound of her familiar voice, Squeeze came racing from upstairs and into her arms.

"Hey, big boy!" she exclaimed, reaching down to pet him as his frame furiously waggled in excitement. "You hungry, baby?"

Squeeze answered with a series of barks that elicited a genuine smile from Puma, something desperately needed during these despairing times.

With Squeeze riding shotgun, Puma pulled into the drive thru of a twenty-four-hour McDonald's.

"Hi, may I take you order?" a woman's voice came over the intercom.

"Yeah, let me get..." Puma paused to peer over at an eager-looking Squeeze, then turned back to the window, "Yeah, let me get four Big Macs and a large water with no ice."

No sooner had the food entered the car than Squeeze began licking his chops. It was as if he'd already known what mouthwatering treat was in store.

"Calm your greedy ass down!" Puma giggled as he continued to grow antsy with anticipation.

After backing into a parking space, Puma removed one of the burgers from the bag and opened its box. By then, Squeeze was nearly in her lap.

Barely chewing, he scarfed down all four sandwiches. He even licked clean the palm of Puma's hand. Before pulling off, she opened the cup's lid and watched with humor as Squeeze thirstily drank from it, spilling water everywhere.

They were back in traffic when Puma could feel herself being watched and turned to lock eyes with her canine companion. Instinctively sensing the sadness by which her soul had been seized, Squeeze maneuvered himself closer and laid his massive head in her lap, gently nudging it against her thigh in a calming manner.

Puma was touched by the dog's gesture. Scratching behind his ear as she witnessed Kavoni do on a number of occasions, she had to force herself not to blink, so as to avoid the leakage of tears from her watery eyes. For even in his absence, her best friend had found a way to provide her with comfort.

I love you, my baby. And I promise to find out what happened. Even if it kills me.

Fumiya Payne

Chapter 27

With the reddish glow of its L.E.D. taillights, a maroon Dodge Charger flew down the darkened highway at nearly triple digits. Behind the smoked glass was King, Double-O, and three of their comrades who'd cross Christ for crumbs. Draped in black from boot-to-beanie, the five villains were vibing to a violent verse by King Von.

"NOW IT'S TIME TO RIDE, IS YOU READY OR WHAT/ CAUGHT A FEW HOMICIDES AND WE AIN'T LETTIN' UP/ I USE TO TRAP WITH THE GANGSTAS AND CLUCKS/ LIKE I'M GIANNIS, I PLAY FOR THEM BUCKS…"

King got off on an exit in a nearby county and wheeled into a truck stop. Crawling through the crowded lot, he found a preferrable parking space and backed in.

"Bro, you sure you know what the fuck you doing?" He turned to question one of the men in the backseat.

Rocking short dreads and a full beard, CJ smiled. "Just chill, my baby. I told you I got my C.D.L."

King scrunched up his face, "Nigga, you ain't even graduate high school, so when the fuck did you get some C.D.L.?"

"I got it in the joint," he said while sliding several tools down his shirt sleeves. "How the fuck you think I got out on early release?"

"CJ, I swear to god, bro," King warned, "if you fuck this lick up, we gon' fall all the way out."

"Ye of little faith." CJ grinned before exiting the car.

With his accomplices paying close attention, CJ approached the driver side of a semi-truck and loudly knocked on its door. After another unanswered knock, he slyly scanned either side of his surroundings before trying the door handle, which to his luck was unlocked. Once inside the semi, CJ quickly removed his tools and used one of them to peel back the dashboard and expose the truck's main circuit breaker. Baring two power wires, he sparked them together and instantly shut down the electronic system. Jamming a flathead screwdriver into the ignition, he attached a pair of channel locks onto its handle. Then, using the leverage of his arm strength and channel locks, he forcefully turned the flathead as if it was a key and broke three pins inside the column.

Inside the Charger, as they looked on in a suspenseful silence, all four men cheered in excitement when the semi rumbled to life.

"That nigga the coldest!" Double-O declared as they trailed the truck out of the lot.

With CJ in the lead as they flew back down the highway, he started honking the horn and elicited a laugh from even King, who felt a fraction of guilt for his doubtful demeanor.

A car thief since kindergarten, CJ - short for Carjack - literally had the tattoo of a screwdriver on his right forearm. Previously sentenced to three years in prison for Grand Theft Auto, he was rumored to have stolen over a hundred cars, thus explaining the origin of his nickname.

Arriving back in Detroit, they paused on a back street to hurriedly transfer their weaponry from the Charger to the truck.

"I need you to be my eyes," Double-O instructed King as he leaned down on the passenger side of the car. "So keep this bitch running and be ready to burn it up."

"But I wanted to go in there with you," King voiced in disappointment.

"Come on, bro, let's go!" CJ yelled out the truck's window.

Double-O held up a finger, then patiently explained to King, "I love you to death, my baby. But this a trip I can't let you take. So just sit tight for the moment, and we'll talk about it later."

King barely nodded, knowing Double-O's decision was based solely on his poor performance from the night he'd gotten shot. So while he couldn't necessarily be mad at his apprehension in allowing him back on the front line, King was now even more determined to prove that he could be as courageous a soldier as any other.

"In a minute, my baby." Double-O patted the hood before jogging off to the truck and climbing in.

With tactical artillery slung around their necks by way of strap attachments, Double-O called for a weapon check as they got within the club's vicinity. In possession of the "Witch Doctor", he had it impregnated with a hundred-round drum.

A firm believer in predestination, Double-O's heart harbored not a hair of fear. If this was the date on which he was destined to die, then so be it. But until that moment arrived, he had every intention of leaving with what he came for: the bag and a bigger body count.

When CJ turned on the street on which the club was located, they adjusted ski masks over their faces and braced themselves for the upcoming impact as he bore down on the gas.

"Mo' murder, no mercy!" one of the hooligans howled just before the semi's nose crashed through the building's front window.

Amid the chaotic screaming and scattering of the crowd inside, the crew leaped out of the truck and fired a volley of warning shots into the ceiling.

"Get the fuck down!"

While the second security guard was nowhere in sight, Double-O spotted one of them crawling toward a shotgun and expelled him from earth with a three-round burst.

After instructing one of his men to murder anyone that moved, Double-O and the others quickly descended the basement steps. As they came upon a closed door, the lead man blew it open with two slugs from a semi auto 12-gauge.

But before they could enter, there was an eruption of gunfire from somewhere inside.

No sooner than the shooter emptied his clip, Double-O unglued his back from the wall, pivoted into the doorway, and opened fire.

With the bucking rifle rapidly spitting out spent shell casings, Double-O was wildly enchanted by the continuous clash between brass and concrete.

Boldly advancing into the room, where roughly a dozen people had fearfully flattened themselves to the floor, Double-O riskily ceased fire in hopes of drawing out the shooter.

From behind an overturned blackjack table came a hail of hollows, several of which hammered near the heart area of Double-O's hoodie.

143

He staggered back several steps as his Kevlar vest absorbed the majority of the impact. Then, ignoring the pain, he raised the rifle above his head and began ripping off rounds while closing in. As the pinkie-size projectiles punched holes through the table, a handgun was hurled over it, followed by a shout of surrender.

Double-O relaxed his trigger finger and ordered for the shooter to show his hands before standing up.

Along with the second security guard was the club's owner.

"Do you know who I am?" the owner questioned with an animal's glare.

Double-O nodded. "A memory." He then ensured that he had a closed-casket funeral.

After his men had collected every coin in sight, as well as what some had slyly concealed on their person, Double-O stood before the security guard.

"You shot me," he calmly commented.

The man splayed his hands in a sensible gesture. "Brah, you would've done the same thing in my position."

"And I'm sure you'd do the same in mine," Double-O coldly replied before sending his soul back to its original owner.

As the trio were making their exit, Double-O stepped over May-May and the two briefly locked eyes. Despite her involvement, she inwardly shivered at the thought of her connection to someone so cold-hearted.

Once back on the ground floor, where his man had murderously maintained crowd control, the four felons fled through the large hole made by the semi.

With sirens wailing in the nearby distance, they hurriedly piled inside the Charger and King screeched out of the parking lot.

They were less than two blocks away when a squad car turned off a side street and headed in their direction.

"Duck down, duck down!" King exclaimed seconds before they rolled past.

Unconsciously holding his breath while watching the rearview, King sighed in relief as the car continued toward the club's location.

Snatching off his mask, CJ reached over the seat to grip King's shoulder in excitement.

"Nigga, you should've seen your boy in there!" he said in praise of Double-O's demonic performance. "This nigga was like a machine up in that bitch!"

In the eyes of his allies, who had just beheld the degree of his savagery, Double-O was the portrait of a pure predator. And they were willing to follow their barbaric prophet in whatever direction led.

King grinned in pride and relief. Proud that his best friend's performance was impressive among their peers. And genuinely relieved that he was able to make it out alive and uninjured.

Double-O turned in his seat. "But just wait till y'all see my brodie in action," he said in reference to King. "Y'all niggas gon' swear he my twin."

Although his statement was not yet true, it still instilled a warm feeling within King's heart. Because to not only share the spotlight, but to also provide him with a certain level of credibility. just further demonstrated the depth of Double-O's love and loyalty.

As the two comrades exchanged a sincere smile, neither knew that their friendship was living on borrowed time.

Fumiya Payne

Chapter 28

Outside an elementary school, Dolphin and his right-hand man, Nooni, leaned against the passenger side of a sparkling sedan. And parked directly behind it was a black SUV, where three killers reclined on the other side of its tinted windows.

As usual, Dolphin's heartbeat hastened in anticipation when the doors blew open and an outpour of children came noisily fleeing to freedom. Routinely scanning the crowd, he spotted the purpose of his life and they both lit up at one another's sight.

"Daddy! Daddy!" the six-year-old cried as her little legs propelled her into her father's extended arms.

Even with the bottom half of his face blanketed by a full beard, the resemblance between them was undeniably strong.

"Hi, baby!" Dolphin sang as he lifted her up, attacking her chubby cheeks with affectionate kisses.

From the styling of her hair to the quality of her clothing, it was quite obvious that Dolphin's daughter was well taken care of - which should be the goal of every able-bodied father.

"So how was school today?" he inquired, referring to students and staff alike. When it came to the little girl in his arms, he wouldn't hesitate to bring it to the doorbell of a student's parent, or the office of a school's principal.

"It was fine. I fell down in gym, but I didn't cry."

After fixing her uninjured elbow with a kiss, Dolphin let her down.

"Hi, Uncle Nooni," she looked up at the tall, brown-skinned man.

"Hi, Teeka." The killer smiled.

"Today my birthday," she informed with a mischievous smile.

"I could've swore your birthday was last week," Nooni said while digging in his pocket.

"Don't be stingy, Uncle. I thought I was your favorite girl."

As he and Dolphin shook their heads in amusement, Nooni handed her a hundred-dollar bill. This being a game they frequently played, Teeka had a birthday at least once a week. And Nooni broke her off with the same amount each time.

With Teeka buckled up in the backseat and Dolphin at the wheel, the two vehicles exited the school's parking lot.

Regardless of his relationship with the streets, Dolphin made time to pick his daughter up from school Monday through Friday. So aside from their time spent together on the weekends, this small sacrifice allowed him to know what was going on with her on a day-to-day basis, whether it was in school, or at home.

"Daddy, I got a joke," Teeka announced.

"A'ight, let me hear it."

"Why did the——" Teeka started giggling before she could finish.

"Come on, girl, let me hear it," Dolphin smiled.

Barely able to subdue her laughter, she asked, "Why did the teddy bear not wanna eat?"

After giving it serious thought, and coming up clueless, Dolphin admitted, "I don't know. Why?"

"Because he was already *stuffed*," Teeka said before again bursting out in laughter.

Even Nooni had to chuckle at that one.

Part of their after-school ritual was stopping for ice cream, which her mother strictly forbade. But with Dolphin being securely wrapped around his daughter's pinkie, along with the maintained secrecy of their lactic affair, her mother's orders were overlooked.

At a parlor in a suburban part of the city, Dolphin and Teeka were enjoying their ice cream cones when she reached up to run a sticky hand over his hair.

"Daddy, can I have the new Cadillac truck?" she slyly slid in.

Knowing she was referring to a power wheel, which she already owned a fleet of, Dolphin said he'd take her to get it once they finished their cones.

Since becoming a member of Kavoni's team, Dolphin had watched his income skyrocket. Whereas he was once only making $5,000 a week, he now saw that within a span of twenty-four hours - which, as a result, enabled him to spoil Teeka rotten.

As he helped Teeka into the backseat, Dolphin received a phone call from one of his workers. While he'd normally ignore it on account of his daughter's presence, instinct encouraged him to answer.

"Yeah, what up?" he greeted in a mildly irritated tone.

"Bro, it's some old nigga saying he need to see you. Talking 'bout it's a emergency."

"Who?"

When Dolphin heard the man state his name in the background, bells of alarm instantly sounded off inside his head. *This can't be good.*

"Bro, he say his name -"

"Aye, where y'all at?" Dolphin interrupted.

Upon his worker disclosing their location, Dolphin told him he was on his way and not to move.

While he genuinely hated to disappoint his daughter, Dolphin could sense this was a situation that required immediate attention. So as he sped toward her mother's condo, he promised Teeka he'd make it up to her the following day.

"But what about my Power Wheel?" She pouted.

Catching a glimpse of her saddened eyes, Dolphin quickly compromised. "Baby, if you can wait till tomorrow, I'll buy you two of 'em. So would you rather have one today, or two tomorrow?"

Teeka wore a thoughtful expression before answering, "Two tomorrow."

"That's my girl." Dolphin smiled.

However, when handing Teeka off to her mother at the front door, Dolphin slipped his "B.M." a small bankroll and instructed her to purchase both Power Wheels before sunset.

"Why you be spoiling her like that?" she questioned in a quarrelsome manner. "Don't you know she already got like six of 'em in the basement?"

"And don't you know it's niggas out here who don't even know they kids!" Dolphin quietly spazzed. "Let alone look after 'em. So shut your ungrateful ass up and let me do me." Turning to walk away, he yelled over his shoulder, "Before sunset!"

Despite their inability to get along, Dolphin's baby mother was fully aware of his intolerance when it came to what he considered mistreatment of his beloved Teeka. So while she might not agree with his constant bestowal of gifts, she'd be sure to have their daughter driving new Power Wheels before sunset.

Reentering the car, Dolphin's energy instantly went from fatherly to felonious.

"I got a feeling we 'bout to go to war," he grimly informed Nooni while racing towards their destination.

Arriving at a convenience store on the west side, Dolphin hurriedly exited the car with his mercenaries marching closely behind.

As Dolphin approached a group of three men, who were standing alongside a white coupe, the troubled expression on the eldest man's face confirmed one of his worse fears.

"What's up, Paulie?" he tensely questioned the older man who had summoned his presence.

Slowly shaking his head, he looked down and mumbled, "They kilt Butchy, nephew."

Although this is what Dolphin had expected to hear, that still didn't prevent his heart from dropping downwards. Butchy wasn't blood-related, but he was the closest thing to a father figure Dolphin had ever had. He'd taught him everything, from being ruthless to responsible. And had it not been for his tutelage, Dolphin doubted he'd still be among the living, which meant the debt ran deep.

"What happened?" Dolphin growled through clenched teeth.

Paulie began to give a detailed account of the robbery that occurred last night at his and Butchy's strip club. "Them muthafuckas drove a semi through the front window, nephew. And they started killing instantly. Our security fought, but them niggas had shit that sounded like it came from the military."

As Dolphin considered the various robbery crews throughout the city, and which ones were capable of carrying out such a bold move, his brain was also racked with a slew of questions. And there was one in particular that couldn't wait.

"Not that I'm mad you survived, but Paulie, how the fuck you manage to be the only one alive to tell this story?"

The man shamefully lowered his head and admitted, "Because I hid soon as I heard the shooting. And even when that nigga murdered Butchy in cold blood, I never made a sound."

While Dolphin eyed the grief-stricken man in contempt for his cowardly conduct, he actually couldn't condemn him for following the cardinal rule of self-preservation. But he could certainly wish that Paulie and his uncle were able to trade places.

Before Paulie's dismissal, he was asked a series of questions pertaining to the robbery, then given instructions to keep an ear to the streets and inform Dolphin of any new information.

"What you think, bro?" Nooni questioned as they watched Paulie pull off in his whip.

Staring after the receding taillights, Dolphin answered, "Whether he involved or not, I think it's only right that Paulie be buried beside Butchy."

Nooni nodded in agreement, for he had been thinking along the same lines. So if Paulie was wise, he'd flee the city tonight. Because if not, he wouldn't live to see tomorrow.

"I know what Butchy meant to you," Nooni commented as he and Dolphin settled back inside the car. "So I promise you, we gon' get to the bottom of it. And when we do..." He turned to give Dolphin direct eye contact, "I'ma murder every man, woman, and child related to that nigga. And that's on God!"

Little did they know, the men responsible were contacts in their phones.

Fumiya Payne

Chapter 29

Inside a darkened garage, Kavoni's arms were distended above his head as he was nakedly suspended from the ceiling by a thick chain. Blindfolded and gagged, he reeked of a repulsive odor that was offensive to even his own nostrils. Since being kidnapped, he'd been forced to have bladder and bowel movements on himself.

With no idea of where he was, the last thing Kavoni recalled was sending Puma the text message. And after a careful reflection of every kill ever committed, he knew the kidnappers could be any number of people. He just prayed it wasn't anyone within his immediate circle, mainly King or Puma. But when considering the corruptive power of the earthly gods Greed and Envy, it would be naive of him to believe that a close comrade was incapable of carrying out such a treacherous act.

The garage door opened and a lone figure quietly entered. Clad in dark clothing and night vision goggles, not an inch of skin was exposed.

Due to the drooping of his head, Kavoni appeared to be asleep. But an unexpected punch to his stomach elicited a muffled groan.

"Figured you were awake," said the unfamiliar voice of a male.

There was a lapse of silence before the kidnapper suddenly lurched forth and struck Kavoni with a series of savage body shots that left him on the verge of vomiting. The gag was removed at the last minute and Kavoni greedily sucked in gulps of oxygen.

"Your people failed to deliver the money," the kidnapper lyingly informed. "Which means you're about to have a real slow and painful death."

They failed to deliver the money? Kavoni repeated to himself. With over a half-million inside the staircase, there could only be one reason for Puma's failure to have paid whatever amount requested. Kavoni was sickened to his stomach at the thought of being betrayed by someone for whom he would've stood before a firing squad.

Clasping his hands behind his back, the kidnapper began circling the darkened garage.

"The average man would've spoken by now," he said in between leisurely strides. "Which suggests that maybe you're not the average man. Or so you think." He paused to inform Kavoni in a sadistic tone, "If properly inflicted, the human body can withstand pain beyond what is imaginable. Pain that would cause a man to betray his own mother. Or in your case, sibling. And I suspect you shall soon find out."

Despite his placement in such a terrifying position, Kavoni's heart retained not a fraction of fear. He knew the connective outcomes to his unlawful lifestyle. Instead, he was plagued by the loathsome feeling of regret. Regret for not noticing that he was obviously being followed prior to the kidnapping. Regret for not paying closer attention to those closest to him. And most of all, regret for the limited amount of time he was in ownership of the crown he'd fought so hard to attain. So in defiance of his dethronement, compliance of any kind was not an option.

Let the pain begin!

He could hear the kidnapper rummaging through what sounded like a toolbox. Mentally preparing himself for the upcoming torture, Kavoni began to recall the merciless beatings he'd suffered on King's behalf as a child. Because if he could endure that at such a tender age, then surely adulthood would allow him to maintain his dignity until admitted into the arms of the afterlife.

When Kavoni heard the footsteps of his captor closing in, he tightened his core in expectancy of a blow. But the man had more sinister plans.

"I'm warning you," he said, placing a high-voltage taser near his testicles. "This will be very painful."

Kavoni screamed from a degree of pain he could've never imagined or possibly prepared for. And before he could fully recover, he was hit with another jolt of electricity, from which he passed out.

He awakened with a sharp jerk and involuntarily yelped.

Toying with his food, the man crackled the taser near Kavoni and watched in amusement as he fearfully flapped around like a fish out of water.

The man literally laughed out loud. "Who would've ever thought the infamous Kavoni McClain would be so scared and helpless. A man who has committed some of the most evil of acts."

With beads of sweat cascading along his trembling torso, Kavoni shouted, "Show your face, coward! Stare me in my eyes like a real killer! Unless you ain't got the stomach for it!"

"We're making progress." The man smiled behind his mask, for these were the first words Kavoni had spoken.

While Kavoni was clueless as to his captor's identity, there were two noticeable things that confirmed he was dealing with a different type of demon: experience and intellect. Because only experience would've allowed his kidnapping to be executed in such a bold and efficient manner. And only intellect would've allowed this man to be so well-spoken.

Thus, Kavoni's prayer for a prompt passing would likely go unanswered. As his captor had promised, he was in for a long and agonizing death.

"I have an idea." The man snickered as he exchanged the taser for a syringe. "One that I think you'll enjoy." He then stepped forward and injected the needle into Kavoni's thigh.

When he awakened, Kavoni surprisingly discovered that he was no longer hanging from the ceiling. With the blindfold also removed, he was now lying on the cold concrete of the garage's floor. However, when he attempted to stand, an intense pain shot through his right arm and he instantly knew the limb was dislocated.

During his state of unconsciousness, the kidnapper had grabbed Kavoni by the wrist, then placed a Timberland boot on his chest for leverage and savagely snatched the arm from within its socket.

"You wanted to see my face," the man said from somewhere to Kavoni's left, "Now here's your chance."

Kavoni whirled in the man's direction, desperate for his eyesight to adjust to the darkness. And despite the disadvantage of having the use of only one arm, he was determined to destroy what he couldn't see.

As the two opponents silently circled the garage, Kavoni was suddenly swept off his feet by a low kick. He cried out in pain when landing on the injured arm.

Quickly climbing back to his feet, he sensed a movement to his left and swung a vicious hook. But he suffered dearly for the miss, and was countered by a crippling punch to his kidney. Then, as his arm reflexively lowered, he was flown backwards by a jarring uppercut.

"It isn't much fun when suffering from a handicap, is it?" the man hissed near Kavoni's ear. "But one must always be willing to digest what they dish out."

Spitting blood, Kavoni gritted his teeth and slowly regained his footing.

Defeat would come only at the hands of death...not submission.

"Who are you?" Kavoni demanded, swaying on unsteady legs.

In a tone cold enough to send chills through a polar bear, the man answered, "The offspring of Satan."

Chapter 30

With Jazz trailing in the Rubicon, Puma was punching the Hellcat down the interstate as she headed to Dearborn, Michigan. In the backseat was a Goyard bag that contained $500,000. This was the thirtieth day from the date of their last heroin shipment, and she was several miles away from honoring Kavoni's monthly arrangement with the Mexicans.

Arriving at the car dealership, Puma parked by the front entrance, just as Kavoni would. In the event of an illness or incarceration, he had prepped for this day in advance.

The usual female employee emerged from the building minutes later and approached the Hellcat. "May I help you with something?"

"Yeah, I'm here on behalf of my brother, Kavoni," she said before reaching in the backseat for the bag. "Unfortunately, he couldn't make it today." Puma held the bag up to the window and assured, "It's all there."

Feigning confusion, the woman refused her offering and took a step back. "Ma'am, I have no idea what you're talking about. So let me check with my supervisor, and I'll return shortly."

In spite of her emotional distress, Puma had managed to maintain business solely on account of Kavoni's expectations. *"Drink water, drive on"*, he had often advised her. A slogan he'd stolen from the military, it taught soldiers to carry on at all costs, which is what she was doing by honoring his monthly arrangement.

Accompanied by a security guard, the woman returned to inform Puma that the manager also had no idea of what she was referring to.

"I'm sorry, ma'am," she added in a firm tone, "but I must now ask you to please leave."

"I understand," Puma replied. "And my apologies."

Their empire constructed on cautionary grounds, the Mexicans weren't taking any chances. So while they were actually aware of who Puma was, as well as her position on Kavoni's team, her presence was not part of the arrangement. And a half-million was only a drop in the bucket, when in comparison to their annual intake.

As Puma was disappointedly driving back to Detroit, the vibration of her phone instantly accelerated her heartbeat, as it often did, in hopes of it being Kavoni. She was listening to the caller with an earnest expression, when the sole of her shoe suddenly pressed the pedal to the floorboard.

"I'm on my way right now," she said before hanging up to hurriedly make another call.

***

The Jeep Rubicon rolled into the Martin Luther King Projects and parked beside a tinted Suburban seated on 26-inch wheels.

As the driver side window of both vehicles simultaneously lowered, a dark-skinned man greeted Jazz with a lift of his ballcap.

"What up, doe?" He smiled, proudly displaying his platinum fronts.

Bypassing frivolous pleasantries, Jazz rudely retorted, "Nigga, do you want the money or not?"

Unsure of their involvement, Puma had refrained from reaching back out to King or Double-O. Instead, she informed a select few of the city's elite that she'd pay fifty grand for any information on Kavoni's kidnapping. Certain that it had taken more than two culprits to carry it out, she was depending on the magnetic pull of greed. And sure enough…

The informant peered beyond Jazz and into the Jeep, as if looking for evidence of the money. She sucked her teeth before lifting a large loaf of money from between her legs.

When he disclosed Kavoni's location, Jazz was unable to mask her shock. *Ain't no fucking way!* Squinting her eyes in skepticism, she asked, "And how I know I ain't walking into no ambush?"

"'Cause that Jeep would've turnt into your casket soon as you rolled your window down," he cockily answered.

Jazz smirked, then lobbed him the loaf.

No sooner had he caught it than Puma rolled from beneath the Rubicon and fired multiple rounds through the Suburban's door.

With blood seeping from several holes in his torso, the man's pupils dilated in fear as a gun's barrel was placed within inches of his eyelids.

"Who else involved?" Puma snarled through gritted teeth.

The man cryingly confessed that he received an anonymous call informing him of Kavoni's location and whether it was accurate or not, he had no clue. "I swear to God, I ain't lying," he pled, grimacing in pain as he held a hand to his stomach.

"You might not be," Puma said before she put his head to bed at point-blank range.

After recovering the money, Puma dove in the Rubicon and Jazz smashed the gas before she could fully close her door.

While lying beneath the Jeep, Puma had also been in disbelief when she heard the location of Kavoni's alleged whereabouts. But if indeed the deceased had delivered accurate information, she just prayed that they would make it in time.

As Jazz turned down the alleyway behind the house on Jo'an, Puma's heart was pumping faster than the strides of a seasoned sprinter. With this house serving solely as a makeshift drug lab, the lack of a fresh shipment had warranted no reason to revisit it. And to think, she'd actually come here the day Kavoni initially went missing.

Slamming on the brakes, Jazz and Puma hurriedly hopped out and ran around to the front of the garage. Its door locked, Puma stepped back and booted it in. With her weapon extended, they cautiously entered the empty enclosure.

Their attention was first drawn to the thick rope that hung from the ceiling. Then, as their eyes traveled downwards, they stared in horror at the amount of blood in which the concrete was covered. And lying in what appeared to be human feces was Kavoni's N.F.L. chain.

Puma was frozen in disbelief. She had combed the city day and night, while all along, her best friend had been right under her nose. She'd been so intimate with her intuition in the past, so she was unable to comprehend its failure in such a time of grave importance.

As she had a flashback of the night Kavoni had praised her for being his counterbalance, then another of his most recent display of emotional attachment, she turned away from Jazz and vomited.

Whatever shred of doubt she had reserved in regard to King and Double-O's involvement had just been washed away. Because who else but an insider would be bold enough to bring Kavoni somewhere so close to home? And who else but an insider would even be aware of this garage's location?

While she'd been hoping for a different outcome, it appeared that Puma would be forced to sign death certificates on two comrades she cared for like siblings.

But it was a dirty game. One designed for only those with hardened hearts and strong stomachs.

Chapter 31

King was carrying several shopping bags as he and Unique leisurely strolled through a mall in Pontiac, Michigan. Clad in matching varsity jackets and powder-blue Nike's, the couple's cuteness elicited complimentary stares of which they were well aware.

Suggesting they grab something to eat, Unique carried their bags to a table in the food court section while he fetched lunch from a pizzeria.

In between bites, Unique laid a hand over King's. "Bae, I'm so proud of you."

"Damn, that's how the breakfast dick got you feeling?" he joked. "All mushy and shit."

She playfully pinched his arm while joining him in laughter.

"But seriously," she continued once the laughter subsided. "As your black Queen, it's my duty to praise you when right, and correct you when wrong. So I gotta admit, you done really stepped up to the plate. And it's not like I'm surprised, but it's just good to see my King carrying himself according to what he is."

King was so unaccustomed to praise that her compliment instantly inflated his confidence to twice its normal size. Out of his entire circle, no one was more emotionally fulfilling than the woman beside him.

With their energy on one accord, Unique grasped his chin and pulled him in for a passionate, pizza-tasting kiss.

Their public display was interrupted by a shapely-built white girl, who was on the arm of a handsome male.

"Unique?"

"Hey, girl!" Unique beamed, rising to greet her with a hug.

The white girl, Paris, was one of the few dancers Unique had befriended at her former place of employment. And despite her milky complexion, Unique swore she was one of the select few who had the soul of a "sista."

"Girl, Rudy really missing you at the club." Paris smiled, speaking in reference to its owner. "You know you was like the main attraction."

Once she and King officially became an item, Unique respectfully sought his opinion in regards to her profession. And upon voicing his disapproval, she immediately offered to quit, with the exception that he suit up and show out. And from the way it appeared, King was on the verge of batting it out of the park.

After the two women shared the latest developments in one another's lives, Paris checked the time before announcing her need to leave. "But it was so good seeing you."

Unique waited several minutes before grabbing her handbag. "I'll be right back, bae. I gotta use the ladies' room."

Inside the women's restroom, where Paris was already present, Unique joined her at the counter.

"Be careful," Paris warned her. "He says it's strong enough to kill half the city."

Exchanging another hug, along with their handbags, they parted ways with a promise to keep in touch.

King and Unique were bubbling with excitement as they exited the mall. The second they climbed back in the cabin of their rental, they eagerly peered inside the handbag. And staring back at them was a rectangular-shaped package that would easily award them $300,000.

Immediately upon King's return with the robbery money from the gambling joint, Unique had reached out to Paris, whose boyfriend she knew was knee-deep in the drug game. After explaining in person what King wanted to purchase, Paris contacted her the following day with instructions to bring $70,000 to the mall in a white handbag. And on account of it not having cameras, the bathroom had been the wisest location for the exchange.

With a skilled chemist on deck, King was ready to sign the contract of a game that could either pass you a luxurious lifestyle or a life sentence - oftentimes both. And it went by the name of "fentanyl."

As King turned out the mall's parking lot, a silver coupe followed suit.

Inside the trailing vehicle was Double-O and May-May, who'd been idling in wait the entire time.

Talkative by nature, May-May was growing frustrated at Double-O's subdued tongue. While she should actually be fearful of being in his presence, there was an unexplainable energy that compelled her to step further into his world. But being a man of few words, it was clear that access was not easily gained. However, the intrigue of his mysterious character caused her to continue trying.

"So, Mr. Double-O..." She smiled. "Is my ugliness the reason you're being so quiet?"

He smirked in amusement, for they both know she was pretty enough to participate in a pageant.

"Okay." May-May grinned. "That's definitely a start."

Based on the way she observed him protectively treat King, May-May could sense that beneath his jagged surface was a softhearted soul. And though she knew not a single word of his back story, her intuition gave her a general idea of how his heart had materialized into a slab of ice.

"Can I ask you a personal question?" May-May inquired. "And you don't have to answer it if you don't want to." It was a shot in the dark, but it was worth an attempt.

Not knowing what to expect, Double-O granted her permission.

"Were you ever self-conscious about being so dark-skinned?"

Although he maintained a neutral expression, Double-O was inwardly stunned by her ability to pinpoint an insecurity it had taken him a long time to overcome, an insecurity that dated back to grade school, when the children would often say mean things and tease him relentlessly.

"Boy you ain't black, you purple," some had hurtfully joked, evoking a room full of laughter. And, *"This dirty, nappy-head-ass nigga gotta be from Africa, y'all. So let's donate him fifteen cents a day."* With no way of knowing how to make it stop, Double-O was forced to endure this type of ridicule for what felt like an eternity.

Until one day, the switch flipped.

Screaming like a wild animal, he publicly pummeled one of his primary oppressors. Then, upon his return to school after a three-day suspension, no one dared openly utter another scornful word. It was in that pivotal moment when he realized the infliction of violence was a means of protecting his fragile feelings. And he had no problem dishing out a beatdown as freely as a pastor did a collection plate at church.

"So I guess you not gon' answer the question?" May-May spoke, bringing his focus back to present day.

As they came to a stop at a red light, Double-O turned to explain with a direct stare. "I don't think you mean no harm, but shorty, you chasing your tail. So let's just keep this shit real simple and business-like."

Unfamiliar with the feeling of rejection, May-May was low-key heated as she crossed her arms in a defensive gesture. "I wasn't suggesting we get in no relationship," she sassily stated, staring straight ahead. "I was just wondering what kind of nigga be around a bad bitch and don't talk. That's some weird shit, if you ask me. But my fault for trying to figure it out."

Double-O scoffed, "Now she got a attitude, 'cause she ain't getting her way."

"I definitely ain't got no attitude," May-May retorted. "In fact, we ain't never gotta exchange another word."

"A'ight, well, say less then. 'Cause I damn sure don't give a fuck."

"A'ight!" May-May shrugged. "And neither do I."

Arriving at King and Unique's new apartment, tension was written all over the faces of Double-O and May-May as they exited the car.

"Girl, what's up?" Unique questioned in concern.

"Not shit!" May-May loudly answered. "Just anxious to get away from these weird-ass niggas!"

As the women walked off, King turned to Double-O and frowned. "Damn, bro, what the fuck happen?"

He waved his hand dismissively. "Mannn, fuck that bitch!"

"Yeah, I understand that part. But I'm saying, what happened?"

"She tried to get all in a nigga head and I shut that shit down. But I'm telling you now, my baby, if that bitch get to acting too weird, she gon' have to take a dirt nap. 'Cause you know she done seen me in action."

A dilemma he hoped to avoid, King was already deliberating on how he would defuse the situation. Unique would have a full-fledged fit if her girl was to suddenly come up missing.

They were walking towards the apartment when Double-O asked King if he'd recently heard from his brother.

"Nah, not for real." He shook his head. "But I've been so caught up in what we doing that I ain't even really been thinking about nothing or nobody else."

Recalling the last conversation he'd had with Puma, Double-O suggested that maybe it was time they reached out. "Because something don't feel right."

Fumiya Payne

Chapter 32

With the closed curtains successfully blocking off all rays of sunlight, Puma was drunkenly seated on her bedroom floor. In briefs and a beater, she held Martha in one hand and a bottle of liquor in the other.

It had been two days since the garage incident, and Puma had yet to summon the will or strength to leave the house. Plagued by a number of emotions, she blamed God, herself, and everyone else for the loss of her best friend.

"How I'm supposed to go on without you?" she tearfully slurred. "Who else gon' understand me?"

Despite the fearless exterior she presented to the world, Puma bore emotional scars from her past that she carefully concealed. And to only one person had she ever grown close enough to reveal secrets that had nearly drove her insane: Kavoni. As someone who'd become like her confidant and balance, his absence would affect her more deeply than anyone could imagine.

Consumed by grief and guilt, Puma had been regretfully reflecting over hers and Kavoni's last disagreement. Though they'd gotten back on good terms, that would forever be one of their final memories. And she couldn't help but think that if her actions had been different, so would the course of his life. *It's all my fault.*

Puma drained what was left in the bottle and hurled it at the screen of her TV, where they both shattered upon impact.

"I know you gon' be mad at me, bro." She racked a live round into the gun's chamber. "But I swear I'd rather burn in hell than to live in this cold world without you."

Choking back a sob, Puma brought the pistol to her temple and lowered her eyelids. While this may have been considered a coward's death, it was the only known escape from her darkened state of distress.

She inhaled a deep breath, clenched her teeth, and pulled the trigger.

Click!

Puma's eyes instantly snapped open at the gun's failure to discharge. With her heartbeat racing, she eyed the loaded weapon in disbelief. In the countless number of drills she had carried out in the field, Martha had *never* misfired. Not even once.

It's not your time, my baby, Kavoni's voice rang loudly in her ears. *So pull yourself together and figure it the fuck out.*

"But I don't know how!" she shouted, throwing Martha across the room in frustration.

Then, as she suddenly recalled a question Kavoni had once posed, Puma buried her face in her palms and shamefully wept.

It had been during one of their weekly visits while he was incarcerated, and Puma was complaining about the difficulty in carrying on without him. After listening with a patient ear, Kavoni's response had been short and sharp. *"Cowards cower, and perseverance prevails. So I'm asking you, my baby...on which side does Puma stand?"*

As she'd done on the day of questioning, Puma found the inner strength and resolve to remove herself from the pool of self-pity. Drying her eyes, she rose to her feet with a renewed sense of energy and trudged to the shower.

While scrubbing away a two-day-old stench, she converted her anguish into anger and started screaming at the top of her lungs.

"Somebody gotta feel my pain," Puma snarled to herself while suiting up in dark-colored garments.

And she knew the perfect person to start with.

***

On the city's west side, a two-door Honda noisily turned into the driveway of a house fit for demolition. Hurriedly exiting the car was a shabbily-dressed man who bore the facial appearance of a dedicated drug addict. No sooner had he unlocked the front door of his one-story shack than he was struck from behind by a hooded figure.

The man emitted a painful groan as he stumbled into the house, where he collapsed onto his hands and knees. But instead of tending to his bleeding wound, he began frantically feeling his hand over the threadbare carpet.

A woman with the figure of a skeleton stormed into the room. He'd been gone entirely too long, and her ashy lips were fixed to fire off a slew of obscenities. But her suspicion was suspended at the sight of her kneeling boyfriend and armed intruder.

The woman cinched her robe tighter, as if something desirable was beneath it. Then, noticing the blood dripping from her boyfriend's head, she rushed over to his aid.

"Charles!" she shrieked, grabbing a dingy towel from the couch to apply over his injury. "Oh my God, baby, are you alright?"

"Naw, bitch!" he angrily snapped. "I lost the fucking dope!"

Despite the presence of a masked gunman, and a wound that would require stitches, the man was more concerned over the gram of heroin he'd lost during the assault.

"Look what you've done!" The woman whirled toward the gunman. "If this about the money we owe——"

Boom! Boom! Boom!

The couple shockingly shrank in fear at the three thunderous gunshots.

Having intentionally missed, the gunman locked the front door, then moved forward until standing over their frightened faces.

With their undivided attention, Puma slowly peeled off the mask to expose the wicked glare of her unblinking eyes.

While the woman expressed no signs of recognition, the man's reaction was the complete opposite.

This was the man Puma had previously followed home and vowed to vengefully return for. The same man who'd cause her to cry then, as well as on a number of occasions in the past. And now the day of reckoning had finally arrived.

Wearing an expression of utter fear, the man looked up at Puma and whispered in disbelief, "Shy'Ann."

At the mention of her real name, Puma was dreadfully reminded of a painful past impossible to forget.

Fumiya Payne

Chapter 33

A young Shy'Ann was contently settled on the floor of her bedroom, playing with her only two Barbie dolls. One she had named Joy, and the other was Star. They were the daughters of loving parents who showered them in an abundance of love, praise, and presents. While this was a far cry from the living conditions within her own home, the illusion of happiness helped her to cope with her hopeless circumstances.

There was a knock at her bedroom door before her mother, Aretha, stepped inside. Her forearms marred by needle marks, the hollow-faced woman weighed no more than her 10-year-old daughter.

Furiously scratching at her arms, Aretha sat on the edge of Shy'Ann's bed and called for the little girl to join her. Abandoning her barbie dolls, Shy'Ann obediently climbed onto the bed.

Aretha ran a rough hand over her daughter's long hair and confided, "I'm sick, Shy. And I don't how much longer I can last if this feeling continues. I really need you, baby."

As she watched her mother through big brown eyes, the little girl had no idea of how she could possibly be of help.

Preying on her childlike innocence, Aretha asked, "Do you love your mama, Shy?"

Although the woman had rare showed her any love or affection, Shy'Ann nodded.

"Well, I need you to do something for me, okay?"

Again, a clueless Shy'Ann nodded.

Aretha leaned over to kiss her cheek before hurriedly leaving the room.

She returned a minute later, accompanied by a partially bald man of average height. And though he wore a friendly expression, there was something about his stare that injected an uneasy feeling into Shy'Ann's heart.

Aretha grasped her by the chin and tilted her head upwards. "I want you to be a good girl and do whatever this man tells you to, you hear me?"

As the feeling of unease had now begun to spread throughout her entire body, Shy'Ann slowly nodded her head.

On her way out of the bedroom, Aretha paused before the man and extended her hand.

Without removing his eyes from Shy'Ann, he reached in his pocket and withdrew a small baggie, which he dropped into Aretha's awaiting palm.

Instantly closing her hand in protection of the precious narcotic, she hustled from the room without once looking back.

He shut the door behind her, then, to Shy'Ann's dismay, he began to get undressed. The flabby skin of his hairy body was repulsive to her underage eyes.

With Shy'Ann being frozen in fear as he nakedly approached her, he took her stillness as a sign of consent and reached out to touch her.

Regaining control of her bodily functions at the last moment, she recoiled from his touch and escaped to a far corner of her room.

"Please leave me alone," she begged in a trembling voice.

While Aretha had pretty much forsaken her during the entirety of her life, this was one of times when Shy'Ann prayed her mother would come to her aid.

Out in the living room, Aretha had one end of a tourniquet clenched between her teeth as she was in the process of tying it around her bony bicep. As she reached for the syringe, she involuntarily flinched at the piercing scream of her only child. With a chance to intervene, she stared from the room to the needle.

Weakly succumbing to the weight of her addiction, Aretha used the injection to numb her hearing to Shy'Ann's heart-wrenching wails.

***

As Puma forcibly repressed the memories of her past, the man mistook her tears of fury for tears of weakness and began to plead.

"I know there ain't nothing I can do to change the past, but I'm truly sorry for what happened. And I gotta live with what I did for the rest of my life. But if your mama hadn't been so persistent about it, I just know I wouldn't have done nothing like that."

Puma had heard enough. For this man to shift the blame for his perversity onto someone else only heightened his sickness. And she'd brought along the perfect cure.

While keeping her gun aimed in their direction, she slipped the backpack off her shoulders and reached inside to remove a set of zip ties. She hurled them at the woman, with instructions to subdue his hands and feet.

When the woman balked in protest, Puma fired a round in her direction.

Now it was the man's turn to weep, as his hands and feet were being bound together. And despite his incessant pleas for Puma to spare his life, his tearful spiel fell on deaf ears.

This was the same man who ruthlessly robbed her of her innocence. The same man who had ensured she'd never bear children, by physically destroying her reproduction system. The same man who caused her to rip off the limbs of her Barbie dolls. The man who had ignored her pleas for mercy over an extended period of time. So no, there would be no admittance of mercy or forgiveness in Puma's heart.

As Puma ordered the woman to roll the man over, she felt a presence to her left and quickly turned.

Peeking around the entranceway of the living room was a dark-skinned girl who appeared to be in her early teens. Cute as a button, she had chubby cheeks and a thick grade of hair that was gathered in two pigtails.

With this being an unexpected problem in Puma's plan, she initially had a sinister thought in regard to solving it. But as she peered into the girl's saddened pupils, she saw a reflection of her own past. And just because there was no one to save her didn't mean she shouldn't prevent the girl from enduring a similar situation, a situation she knew that had the ability to devastate and dismantle.

Stepping in front of the girl so as to obstruct her view of the man and woman, Puma locked eyes with her and asked if she had ever been the victim of sexual assault.

"I've been there," Puma admitted, "So I can definitely relate. And I won't judge you."

When the girl answered with a subtle nod, Puma could feel her blood beginning to boil.

She removed her car keys from her pants pocket and tossed them to the girl. "It's a purple car down the street. I want you to go wait for me in there."

The woman yelled for her not to move, and Puma raced over to shove Martha in her ragged mouth. "Say another word and it'll be your last, bitch!"

Once the girl had left the house, Puma imploringly asked the woman how could she allow the indecent mistreatment of that beautiful baby. How could she allow anything to outweigh her desire to love and protect her? As Puma realized those were questions she always yearned to ask her own mother, the woman's face suddenly transformed into Aretha's.

Becoming enraged, Puma grabbed her by what little hair she has and began violently striking her with the gun. "I HATE YOU! I HATE YOU! I HATE YOU!" she repeatedly screamed with each brutal blow.

The woman bore a lifeless appearance when Puma tiredly tossed her aside.

Now for the main course.

Puma breathlessly reached back inside the backpack and removed the biggest strap-on she owned. And she purposely forgot to bring the lube.

"I'ma make you feel the pain I felt," she snarled at the man before snatching down his pants.

Inside the Hellcat, the girl was crouched in its backseat.

At the faint sound of multiple gunshots, she peeked out the rear windshield and saw muzzle flashes through the front window of her former home.

She quickly ducked down as Puma came jogging back to the car, but not before her observant eyes noticed that she no longer had the backpack.

As Puma slipped behind the wheel, she peered over her shoulder while bringing the Hemi to life. "You good?"

Because she could sense that she was in good hands, the girl was unafraid of the murderous glare in Puma's eyes and answered with a subtle nod.

Then, to Puma's surprise, she softly spoke.

"What about Auntie?" she asked with a peculiar gleam in her eyes.

Providing the answer she knew the girl was secretly seeking, Puma replied, "You better off without her."

As they slowly rolled past, both women's eyes indifferently observed the small house, which was now engulfed in a blazing fire.

Fumiya Payne

Chapter 34
7:30 a.m.

"She's a runner, she's a track star/ she gon' run away when it gets hard/ she can't take the pain, she can't get scarred/ she hurts anyone that gets involved..."

Inside a Chevy Impala, an attractive young woman was singing along with Mooski's hit single as she headed to work. A track star herself, she could personally relate to the validity of the song's lyrics.

She suddenly came upon a detour sign signaling that the road up ahead was closed off for construction work. Pausing at the next intersection, she pondered over the quickest route to her job. *The E-way,* she concluded to herself before turning down a back street.

When she briefly removed her eyes from the road to glance down at the time, she looked back up and screamed. Jerking the wheel to her left, she slammed on her brakes and barely avoided a head-on collision with a utility pole.

"Oh my God," she panted in relief, gratefully pressing her head into the steering wheel. Her heart pounding, she then nervously scanned the area before her gaze slowly slid toward the rearview mirror. While she strongly considered driving off, something compelled her to exit the car.

She covered her mouth in shock at the sight of a naked male lying in the street, as if he'd been thrown out like an unwanted appliance. Edging closer towards the dead body, she noticed that the face was swollen beyond recognition and the right arm was grotesquely bent. And while his skin was a canvas of prison ink, there was a design in particular that caught her eye.

Emblazoned over his throat was the large tattoo of an N.F.L. logo.

To Be Continued...
Salute my Savagery 2
Coming Soon

Fumiya Payne

An original poem is enclosed on the following page

-Self Love-

Is self-preservation not a rule by which all mankind must constantly abide? Is self-worth not more valuable than a priceless pearl its possessor would protectively hide?

So march with self-confidence as you navigate throughout this self-centered globe... sip on the water of self-discipline as you engage in the exercise of self-control.

Stop! with self-inflicted blows that fracture the bones of your self-esteem... when self-doubt is only a roadblock on your roadway to becoming a Queen.

Bypass negativity as you recline behind the wheel of self-reliance....
and readily remove from your presence the passenger who is opposed to compliance.

For within your palm is the inspiring portrait of self-sufficiency... so if self-employment yields enjoyment, then I suggest you invest in the stocks of consistency.

Learn that voters are needless, when you've been self-elected to preside over your dauntless domain... you could scream your achievements, but no announcement is needed for something self-proclaimed.

You're an earthly star, so why be self-conscious of your figure that's not symmetrically slim? You were perfectly carved, so why in the pool of self-pity do you continuously swim?

You were prescribed with a prosperous spirit from the Heavens above... but you must first acknowledge that little is accomplished without the accomplice of self-love!

Yours truly,
Fumiya Payne

Lock Down Publications and Ca$h Presents assisted
publishing packages.

BASIC PACKAGE $499
Editing
Cover Design
Formatting

UPGRADED PACKAGE $800
Typing
Editing
Cover Design
Formatting

ADVANCE PACKAGE $1,200
Typing
Editing
Cover Design
Formatting
Copyright registration
Proofreading
Upload book to Amazon

LDP SUPREME PACKAGE $1,500
Typing
Editing
Cover Design
Formatting
Copyright registration
Proofreading
Set up Amazon account
Upload book to Amazon
Advertise on LDP Amazon and Facebook page

***Other services available upon request. Additional charges may apply
Lock Down Publications
P.O. Box 944
Stockbridge, GA 30281-9998
Phone # 470 303-9761

Submission Guideline

Submit the first three chapters of your completed manuscript to ldpsubmissions@gmail.com, subject line: Your book's title. The manuscript must be in a .doc file and sent as an attachment. Document should be in Times New Roman, double spaced and in size 12 font. Also, provide your synopsis and full contact information. If sending multiple submissions, they must each be in a separate email.

Have a story but no way to send it electronically? You can still submit to LDP/Ca$h Presents. Send in the first three chapters, written or typed, of your completed manuscript to:

LDP: Submissions Dept
Po Box 944
Stockbridge, Ga 30281

DO NOT send original manuscript. Must be a duplicate.

Provide your synopsis and a cover letter containing your full contact information.

Thanks for considering LDP and Ca$h Presents.

<u>NEW RELEASES</u>

BLOOD OF A GOON by ROMELL TUKES

THE COCAINE PRINCESS 8 by KING RIO

THE MURDER QUEENS 3 by MICHAEL GALLON

GORILLAZ IN THE TRENCHES 3 by SAYNOMORE

SALUTE MY SAVAGERY by FUMIYA PAYNE

Salute my Savagery

Coming Soon from Lock Down Publications/Ca$h Presents
BLOOD OF A BOSS **VI**

SHADOWS OF THE GAME II

TRAP BASTARD II

By **Askari**

LOYAL TO THE GAME **IV**

By **T.J. & Jelissa**

TRUE SAVAGE **VIII**

MIDNIGHT CARTEL IV

DOPE BOY MAGIC IV

CITY OF KINGZ III

NIGHTMARE ON SILENT AVE II

THE PLUG OF LIL MEXICO II

CLASSIC CITY II

By **Chris Green**

BLAST FOR ME **III**

A SAVAGE DOPEBOY III

CUTTHROAT MAFIA III

DUFFLE BAG CARTEL VII

HEARTLESS GOON VI

By **Ghost**

A HUSTLER'S DECEIT III

KILL ZONE II

BAE BELONGS TO ME III

TIL DEATH II

By **Aryanna**

KING OF THE TRAP III

By **T.J. Edwards**

GORILLAZ IN THE BAY V

3X KRAZY III

STRAIGHT BEAST MODE III

De'Kari

KINGPIN KILLAZ IV

STREET KINGS III

PAID IN BLOOD III

CARTEL KILLAZ IV

DOPE GODS III

Hood Rich

SINS OF A HUSTLA II

ASAD

YAYO V

Bred In The Game 2

S. Allen

THE STREETS WILL TALK II

By Yolanda Moore

SON OF A DOPE FIEND III

HEAVEN GOT A GHETTO III

SKI MASK MONEY III

By Renta

LOYALTY AIN'T PROMISED III

By Keith Williams

I'M NOTHING WITHOUT HIS LOVE II

SINS OF A THUG II

TO THE THUG I LOVED BEFORE II

IN A HUSTLER I TRUST II

By Monet Dragun

QUIET MONEY IV

EXTENDED CLIP III

THUG LIFE IV

By **Trai'Quan**

Salute my Savagery

THE STREETS MADE ME IV
By **Larry D. Wright**
IF YOU CROSS ME ONCE III
ANGEL V
By **Anthony Fields**
THE STREETS WILL NEVER CLOSE IV
By K'ajji
HARD AND RUTHLESS III
KILLA KOUNTY IV
By Khufu
MONEY GAME III
By Smoove Dolla
JACK BOYS VS DOPE BOYS IV
A GANGSTA'S QUR'AN V
COKE GIRLZ II
COKE BOYS II
LIFE OF A SAVAGE V
CHI'RAQ GANGSTAS V
SOSA GANG III
BRONX SAVAGES II
BODYMORE KINGPINS II
BLOOD OF A GOON II
By Romell Tukes
MURDA WAS THE CASE III
Elijah R. Freeman
AN UNFORESEEN LOVE IV
BABY, I'M WINTERTIME COLD III
By **Meesha**

QUEEN OF THE ZOO III

Fumiya Payne

By **Black Migo**
CONFESSIONS OF A JACKBOY III
By Nicholas Lock
KING KILLA II
By Vincent "Vitto" Holloway
BETRAYAL OF A THUG III
By Fre$h
THE BIRTH OF A GANGSTER III
By Delmont Player
TREAL LOVE II
By Le'Monica Jackson
FOR THE LOVE OF BLOOD III
By Jamel Mitchell
RAN OFF ON DA PLUG II
By Paper Boi Rari
HOOD CONSIGLIERE III
By Keese
PRETTY GIRLS DO NASTY THINGS II
By Nicole Goosby
LOVE IN THE TRENCHES II
By Corey Robinson
IT'S JUST ME AND YOU II
By Ah'Million
FOREVER GANGSTA III
By Adrian Dulan
THE COCAINE PRINCESS IX
By King Rio
CRIME BOSS II
Playa Ray
LOYALTY IS EVERYTHING III

188

Salute my Savagery

Molotti
HERE TODAY GONE TOMORROW II
By Fly Rock
REAL G'S MOVE IN SILENCE II
By Von Diesel
GRIMEY WAYS IV
By Ray Vinci
SALUTE MY SAVAGERY II
By Fumiya Payne

Available Now

RESTRAINING ORDER **I & II**
By **CA$H & Coffee**
LOVE KNOWS NO BOUNDARIES **I II & III**
By **Coffee**
RAISED AS A GOON I, II, III & IV
BRED BY THE SLUMS I, II, III
BLAST FOR ME I & II
ROTTEN TO THE CORE I II III
A BRONX TALE I, II, III
DUFFLE BAG CARTEL I II III IV V VI
HEARTLESS GOON I II III IV V
A SAVAGE DOPEBOY I II
DRUG LORDS I II III
CUTTHROAT MAFIA I II

Fumiya Payne

KING OF THE TRENCHES
By **Ghost**
LAY IT DOWN **I & II**
LAST OF A DYING BREED I II
BLOOD STAINS OF A SHOTTA I & II III
By **Jamaica**
LOYAL TO THE GAME I II III
LIFE OF SIN I, II III
By **TJ & Jelissa**
BLOODY COMMAS I & II
SKI MASK CARTEL I II & III
KING OF NEW YORK I II,III IV V
RISE TO POWER I II III
COKE KINGS I II III IV V
BORN HEARTLESS I II III IV
KING OF THE TRAP I II
By **T.J. Edwards**
IF LOVING HIM IS WRONG...I & II
LOVE ME EVEN WHEN IT HURTS I II III
By **Jelissa**
WHEN THE STREETS CLAP BACK I & II III
THE HEART OF A SAVAGE I II III IV
MONEY MAFIA I II
LOYAL TO THE SOIL I II III
By **Jibril Williams**
A DISTINGUISHED THUG STOLE MY HEART I II & III
LOVE SHOULDN'T HURT I II III IV
RENEGADE BOYS I II III IV
PAID IN KARMA I II III
SAVAGE STORMS I II III

190

Salute my Savagery

AN UNFORESEEN LOVE I II III

BABY, I'M WINTERTIME COLD I II

By **Meesha**

A GANGSTER'S CODE I &, II III

A GANGSTER'S SYN I II III

THE SAVAGE LIFE I II III

CHAINED TO THE STREETS I II III

BLOOD ON THE MONEY I II III

A GANGSTA'S PAIN I II III

By J-Blunt

PUSH IT TO THE LIMIT

By **Bre' Hayes**

BLOOD OF A BOSS **I, II, III, IV, V**

SHADOWS OF THE GAME

TRAP BASTARD

By **Askari**

THE STREETS BLEED MURDER **I, II & III**

THE HEART OF A GANGSTA I II& III

By **Jerry Jackson**

CUM FOR ME I II III IV V VI VII VIII

An **LDP Erotica Collaboration**

BRIDE OF A HUSTLA **I II & II**

THE FETTI GIRLS **I, II& III**

CORRUPTED BY A GANGSTA I, II III, IV

BLINDED BY HIS LOVE

THE PRICE YOU PAY FOR LOVE I, II ,III

DOPE GIRL MAGIC I II III

By **Destiny Skai**

WHEN A GOOD GIRL GOES BAD

By **Adrienne**

Fumiya Payne

THE COST OF LOYALTY I II III
By Kweli
A GANGSTER'S REVENGE **I II III & IV**
THE BOSS MAN'S DAUGHTERS I II III IV V
A SAVAGE LOVE **I & II**
BAE BELONGS TO ME I II
A HUSTLER'S DECEIT I, II, III
WHAT BAD BITCHES DO I, II, III
SOUL OF A MONSTER I II III
KILL ZONE
A DOPE BOY'S QUEEN I II III
TIL DEATH
By **Aryanna**
A KINGPIN'S AMBITON
A KINGPIN'S AMBITION **II**
I MURDER FOR THE DOUGH
By **Ambitious**
TRUE SAVAGE I II III IV V VI VII
DOPE BOY MAGIC I, II, III
MIDNIGHT CARTEL I II III
CITY OF KINGZ I II
NIGHTMARE ON SILENT AVE
THE PLUG OF LIL MEXICO II
CLASSIC CITY
By **Chris Green**
A DOPEBOY'S PRAYER
By **Eddie "Wolf" Lee**
THE KING CARTEL **I, II & III**
By **Frank Gresham**
THESE NIGGAS AIN'T LOYAL **I, II & III**

Salute my Savagery

By **Nikki Tee**
GANGSTA SHYT **I II &III**
By **CATO**
THE ULTIMATE BETRAYAL
By **Phoenix**
BOSS'N UP **I , II & III**
By **Royal Nicole**
I LOVE YOU TO DEATH
By **Destiny J**
I RIDE FOR MY HITTA
I STILL RIDE FOR MY HITTA
By **Misty Holt**
LOVE & CHASIN' PAPER
By **Qay Crockett**
TO DIE IN VAIN
SINS OF A HUSTLA
By **ASAD**
BROOKLYN HUSTLAZ
By **Boogsy Morina**
BROOKLYN ON LOCK I & II
By **Sonovia**
GANGSTA CITY
By **Teddy Duke**
A DRUG KING AND HIS DIAMOND I & II III
A DOPEMAN'S RICHES
HER MAN, MINE'S TOO I, II
CASH MONEY HO'S
THE WIFEY I USED TO BE I II
PRETTY GIRLS DO NASTY THINGS
By Nicole Goosby

Fumiya Payne

TRAPHOUSE KING **I II & III**

KINGPIN KILLAZ I II III

STREET KINGS I II

PAID IN BLOOD **I II**

CARTEL KILLAZ I II III

DOPE GODS I II

By **Hood Rich**

LIPSTICK KILLAH **I, II, III**

CRIME OF PASSION I II & III

FRIEND OR FOE I II III

By **Mimi**

STEADY MOBBN' **I, II, III**

THE STREETS STAINED MY SOUL I II III

By **Marcellus Allen**

WHO SHOT YA **I, II, III**

SON OF A DOPE FIEND I II

HEAVEN GOT A GHETTO I II

SKI MASK MONEY I II

Renta

GORILLAZ IN THE BAY **I II III IV**

TEARS OF A GANGSTA I II

3X KRAZY I II

STRAIGHT BEAST MODE I II

DE'KARI

TRIGGADALE I II III

MURDAROBER WAS THE CASE I II

Elijah R. Freeman

GOD BLESS THE TRAPPERS I, II, III

THESE SCANDALOUS STREETS I, II, III

FEAR MY GANGSTA I, II, III IV, V

Salute my Savagery

THESE STREETS DON'T LOVE NOBODY I, II

BURY ME A G I, II, III, IV, V

A GANGSTA'S EMPIRE I, II, III, IV

THE DOPEMAN'S BODYGAURD I II

THE REALEST KILLAZ I II III

THE LAST OF THE OGS I II III

Tranay Adams

THE STREETS ARE CALLING

Duquie Wilson

MARRIED TO A BOSS I II III

By Destiny Skai & Chris Green

KINGZ OF THE GAME I II III IV V VI VII

CRIME BOSS

Playa Ray

SLAUGHTER GANG I II III

RUTHLESS HEART I II III

By Willie Slaughter

FUK SHYT

By Blakk Diamond

DON'T F#CK WITH MY HEART I II

By Linnea

ADDICTED TO THE DRAMA I II III

IN THE ARM OF HIS BOSS II

By Jamila

YAYO I II III IV

A SHOOTER'S AMBITION I II

BRED IN THE GAME

By S. Allen

TRAP GOD I II III

RICH $AVAGE I II III

Fumiya Payne

MONEY IN THE GRAVE I II III
By Martell Troublesome Bolden
FOREVER GANGSTA I II
GLOCKS ON SATIN SHEETS I II
By Adrian Dulan
TOE TAGZ I II III IV
LEVELS TO THIS SHYT I II
IT'S JUST ME AND YOU
By Ah'Million
KINGPIN DREAMS I II III
RAN OFF ON DA PLUG
By Paper Boi Rari
CONFESSIONS OF A GANGSTA I II III IV
CONFESSIONS OF A JACKBOY I II
By Nicholas Lock
I'M NOTHING WITHOUT HIS LOVE
SINS OF A THUG
TO THE THUG I LOVED BEFORE
A GANGSTA SAVED XMAS
IN A HUSTLER I TRUST
By Monet Dragun
CAUGHT UP IN THE LIFE I II III
THE STREETS NEVER LET GO I II III
By Robert Baptiste
NEW TO THE GAME I II III
MONEY, MURDER & MEMORIES I II III
By **Malik D. Rice**
LIFE OF A SAVAGE I II III IV
A GANGSTA'S QUR'AN I II III IV
MURDA SEASON I II III

196

Salute my Savagery

GANGLAND CARTEL I II III

CHI'RAQ GANGSTAS I II III IV

KILLERS ON ELM STREET I II III

JACK BOYZ N DA BRONX I II III

A DOPEBOY'S DREAM I II III

JACK BOYS VS DOPE BOYS I II III

COKE GIRLZ

COKE BOYS

SOSA GANG I II

BRONX SAVAGES

BODYMORE KINGPINS

BLOOD OF A GOON

By Romell Tukes

LOYALTY AIN'T PROMISED I II

By Keith Williams

QUIET MONEY I II III

THUG LIFE I II III

EXTENDED CLIP I II

A GANGSTA'S PARADISE

By **Trai'Quan**

THE STREETS MADE ME I II III

By **Larry D. Wright**

THE ULTIMATE SACRIFICE I, II, III, IV, V, VI

KHADIFI

IF YOU CROSS ME ONCE I II

ANGEL I II III IV

IN THE BLINK OF AN EYE

By **Anthony Fields**

THE LIFE OF A HOOD STAR

By Ca$h & Rashia Wilson

THE STREETS WILL NEVER CLOSE I II III

By K'ajji

CREAM I II III

THE STREETS WILL TALK

By Yolanda Moore

NIGHTMARES OF A HUSTLA I II III

By King Dream

CONCRETE KILLA I II III

VICIOUS LOYALTY I II III

By Kingpen

HARD AND RUTHLESS I II

MOB TOWN 251

THE BILLIONAIRE BENTLEYS I II III

REAL G'S MOVE IN SILENCE

By Von Diesel

GHOST MOB

Stilloan Robinson

MOB TIES I II III IV V VI

SOUL OF A HUSTLER, HEART OF A KILLER I II

GORILLAZ IN THE TRENCHES I II III

By SayNoMore

BODYMORE MURDERLAND I II III

THE BIRTH OF A GANGSTER I II

By Delmont Player

FOR THE LOVE OF A BOSS

By C. D. Blue

MOBBED UP I II III IV

THE BRICK MAN I II III IV V

THE COCAINE PRINCESS I II III IV V VI VII VIII

By King Rio

Salute my Savagery

KILLA KOUNTY I II III IV
By Khufu
MONEY GAME I II
By Smoove Dolla
A GANGSTA'S KARMA I II III
By FLAME
KING OF THE TRENCHES I II III
by **GHOST & TRANAY ADAMS**
QUEEN OF THE ZOO I II
By **Black Migo**
GRIMEY WAYS I II III
By Ray Vinci
XMAS WITH AN ATL SHOOTER
By Ca$h & Destiny Skai
KING KILLA
By Vincent "Vitto" Holloway
BETRAYAL OF A THUG I II
By Fre$h
THE MURDER QUEENS I II III
By Michael Gallon
TREAL LOVE
By Le'Monica Jackson
FOR THE LOVE OF BLOOD I II
By Jamel Mitchell
HOOD CONSIGLIERE I II
By Keese
PROTÉGÉ OF A LEGEND I II III
LOVE IN THE TRENCHES
By Corey Robinson
BORN IN THE GRAVE I II III

Fumiya Payne

By Self Made Tay

MOAN IN MY MOUTH

By XTASY

TORN BETWEEN A GANGSTER AND A GENTLEMAN

By J-BLUNT & Miss Kim

LOYALTY IS EVERYTHING I II

Molotti

HERE TODAY GONE TOMORROW

By Fly Rock

PILLOW PRINCESS

By S. Hawkins

NAÏVE TO THE STREETS

WOMEN LIE MEN LIE I II III

GIRLS FALL LIKE DOMINOS

STACK BEFORE YOU SPURLGE

FIFTY SHADES OF SNOW I II III

By A. Roy Milligan

SALUTE MY SAVAGERY

By Fumiya Payne

BOOKS BY LDP'S CEO, CA$H

TRUST IN NO MAN

TRUST IN NO MAN 2

TRUST IN NO MAN 3

BONDED BY BLOOD

SHORTY GOT A THUG

THUGS CRY

THUGS CRY 2

THUGS CRY 3

TRUST NO BITCH

TRUST NO BITCH 2

TRUST NO BITCH 3

TIL MY CASKET DROPS

RESTRAINING ORDER

RESTRAINING ORDER 2

IN LOVE WITH A CONVICT

LIFE OF A HOOD STAR

XMAS WITH AN ATL SHOOTER

Fumiya Payne